Falling for the Deputy

Hopeless Romantics of Willow Ridge
#4

Karen McCullough

ACKNOWLEDGEMENTS

Many people contributed to making this book possible, but there are two special women who helped shape and guide the story into its current format.

My sister Barbara, the real-life inspiration for Barbara Wilton, spent a lot of time reading the manuscript and explaining all the bank procedures I got wrong. I've done my best to follow her guidance in reworking them. She caught several other embarrassing bloopers in the story as well. If I've messed up the bank procedures that's totally on me.

My daughter Sarah is the best editor any author could hope for. She made any number of suggestions to help deepen and enrich the emotional elements of the story and caught more than a few typos.

I'm deeply grateful to both.

I also have to thank several members of the CrimeSceneWriters group for help with the law enforcement elements of the story. Again, any mistakes in that area are my own.

Finally, I owe my husband a large debt for his support of my writing career all these years!

About This Book

Can a group of hopeless romantics finally find love? Or are they destined always to be a bridesmaid and never the bride?

After losing at love twice, Barbara Wilton needs a change, some place far from her home in Boston, so she takes a position as manager of a small branch bank in Willow Ridge, Georgia. She's done with relationships and ready to concentrate on her career. The experience in Willow Ridge will help her move forward in the banking industry, but she doesn't plan to stay there permanently. Nevertheless an invitation to join the Hopeless Romantics book club, a position on a planning committee, helping a little league team that needs coaching, and being adopted by a stray dog begin to wind her into the community.

Chris Harper was a police officer in Charlotte until his marriage fell apart. With his mother and elderly aunt in deteriorating health, Chris returns home to Willow Ridge to help them and takes a job as chief deputy to the local sheriff. The wound left by his failed marriage is still raw and, despite his mother's nagging, he's not interested in pursuing any relationship, even with the attractive new bank manager.

Fate, helped by a few local residents, conspires to push Barbara and Chris together. They meet during a false alarm at the bank and then he assists her with a car problem. But when his aunt receives a foreclosure notice on her house, Chris is angry with Barbara for not warning him that his aunt was behind on her payments.

She agrees to help him work out the problem with the bank but the deeper issues between them keep flaring. Can two wary, wounded people learn to trust again and find happiness together? Find out in this sweet, second chance romance.

CHAPTER 1

Chief Deputy Chris Harper held the phone a few inches from his ear, but he could still hear the older lady's shrill screaming. "You've got to do something," she demanded. "I'm getting so sick and tired of that mutt digging up my garden."

He brought the phone a couple of inches closer. "You've tried to talk to your neighbor about it?"

"Only half a dozen times. He still lets the dog run around loose. If you don't do something soon, I'm gonna get that old shotgun Pete left and take care of the mutt myself."

Chris clapped the phone back to his ear. "Please don't do that, ma'am! We'll have someone talk to your neighbor about controlling his dog." He scribbled a note on the pad next to the computer.

"You do that. Soon or I'll..." She continued on.

Another deputy burst through his office door, breathing hard. "Situation at the bank! The alarm's going off."

"I have to go," he said to the woman on the phone. "Emergency."

He ended the call without waiting for her response. "What's going on?"

"All I know is the alarm is going off at the bank. What do we do?"

The County Sheriff, Will McCormick, was recovering from surgery on his back. Since Chris was the Chief Deputy, second-in-command, this was his problem. "See how many units dispatch can send. I'm on the way. But it's quiet mode and no one approaches until I get there and give the word. Surround and observe unless there's an immediate threat. Call the bank manager and have him meet us there."

He noted the time. Eight twenty-eight in the evening. Odds were better than even this was a false alarm, likely a cleaning crew that forgot to enter the code. He'd seen it happen several times when he worked with the police department in Charlotte.

He grabbed his hat and keys and raced out to the parking lot. The moment he hit the humid, late June Georgia air, he began sweating. Gary, the very young deputy who'd alerted him, followed him out. "Dispatch says they have two units responding besides us."

"Ride with me," he suggested to Gary. The kid couldn't be more than twenty, but he was bright enough to show promise.

"Do you think it's a real robbery?" Gary asked as they cruised out of the parking lot for the five-block trip to Willow Ridge's only branch bank.

"Probably not, but I never assume anything.

More often than not, these are false alarms, but you never approach it that way until you know for sure. Check the computer for more details," he said.

The young man did. "Dispatch says it's a rear door alarm going off. One unit is already there. He says there's no sign of a disturbance from the front but he's waiting further directions."

"Good. Tell dispatch to have the next unit go around back. Let us know if there are any vehicles parked there."

Gary did as directed. Just as they pulled up in front of the bank, the dispatcher informed them the second unit was in back and reported a van parked there bearing the logo of a local cleaning service.

"Figures," Chris said. He parked, got out quietly, and walked over to the other marked car. Daylight was fading, but enough light remained to let them see reasonably well. "Cover me. I'm going to the door." He activated his shoulder microphone so dispatch and the other deputies would hear whatever he said.

He crossed the street to the front door, careful to stay out of the line of sight of anyone inside. Keeping to the side, he tapped on the glass door and called, loudly, "Sheriff's department. Come out with your hands over your head." He put his hand on his holstered pistol but didn't draw it.

Nothing happened for a couple of moments except for the beads of sweat running down his back. Then a scuffle of footsteps and the snick of the door latch preceded the appearance of a middle-aged man and woman. Both wore the uniforms of the cleaning service named on the van out back and held their hands on their heads.

"Don't shoot," the man said, sounding near panic. "We're just the cleaners. Don't shoot!"

"We won't as long you keep your hands up."

A Lexus SUV pulled to the curb right in front of the bank and stopped. Chris signaled for Gary to join him, and the young deputy got out of the car and crossed the street. "Keep an eye on them," Chris directed. He walked over to the SUV as the driver's door opened.

The woman who stepped out was younger than he would've expected of a branch manager, probably late twenties, early thirties at most. She wore shorts and a tee shirt that showed off a nicely curved figure. In the fading twilight he noted medium brown hair that fell in waves around an oval face with large dark eyes and a pert nose. He could've happily spent the rest of the evening staring at her, but he was on duty, so he shook himself out of the bemusement.

"Deputy Chris Harper," he identified himself. "Are you the bank manager?"

"Yes. Barbara Wilton. What's going on? I got a call that there was a break-in."

He turned to look at the two people standing on the sidewalk with their hands on their heads before facing the woman again. "We responded to an alarm going off. But I think it was the cleaning crew."

"Oh, heck," she said. "Yeah, probably. This is their time window." She had a strong northern accent.

"Dale's Cleaning Service?"

"That's the right company," she agreed.

"Can you identify these two?"

"I've never met any of their employees."

"Okay, give me a minute to verify them."

He took the names of the two people and asked dispatch to check with the cleaning company about them. While they waited, he asked Miss Wilton about their instructions to the cleaning company. "I gather you must've shared an alarm code with them, since this doesn't happen every night?"

"The company has a special code to use. I wonder if one or both of them are new employees who either didn't understand the instructions or didn't think they were important?"

"Very likely," he said. "You might want to have a talk with the company."

"I will."

He got word back verifying that the two people who'd been in the bank were employees of the cleaning service.

At that point, he sent the other deputies on their way, including Gary, who went along with one of the others to a traffic accident just reported. He told the cleaning crew they could return to work but warned them to check in with their employers about the proper procedure for disabling and then re-enabling the alarm.

"They probably don't know how to reset it behind them either," Barbara said. "I'd better wait here until they're finished and then lock up behind them."

"Can you shut it off right now?" he asked.

"Sure."

"Let's do that, and I'll wait with you until the cleaners are finished. I don't like the idea of you being alone here in the bank in the dark."

"That's kind of you, Deputy Harper. It saves me having to call someone else to come and close up again with me."

Her smile penetrated and touched something deep inside him. Something he'd thought dead since Britt told him she wanted a divorce. Something that should probably remain dead.

"Part of the job." He nodded toward the building. "Let's go shut off the alarm for now."

They followed the cleaning crew back inside. While the man resumed vacuuming and the woman dusted shelves, Barbara took him into the back where the alarm reset was located. Once she'd handled that, she got sodas for each of them from the break room and suggested they wait in her office.

"Since you insist on waiting with me," she said. "We might as well be comfortable."

"Thanks." Two upholstered chairs flanked a low table in a corner of her office, and she sat in one of them, inviting him to take the other. Better light just enhanced how attractive she was. It made him uneasy.

"I'm sorry if I'm keeping you from your work, Deputy Harper."

He laughed. "First, it's Chris. At least as long as I'm not arresting you. I trust I won't have any need to do that!"

"I certainly hope so, too."

"It's been a pretty quiet night, so far. The alarm interrupted my phone conversation with an elderly woman threatening to shoot her neighbor's dog because he was digging up her garden."

"You discouraged the attempt?"

"I suspect if she tried, she'd manage to shoot up everything but the dog."

She laughed this time, and the way it lit her face pushed the dart of attraction deeper into his chest. He struggled to keep his breath even.

"Are you new in town, Deputy Harper? I don't think I've seen you before. Not that I actually have much interaction with law enforcement personally, but deputies do come into the bank occasionally."

"Yes and no on the new in town. I actually grew up here, but after college I got a job with the police department in Charlotte. I only moved back a few months ago. My dad died several years back and my mom's getting older and having some health issues. My aunt Ruth, too. They need someone close by, so I moved back."

"You're an only child?"

"I have a sister, but she's married and has a family. They're in Wilmington."

"Delaware?" she asked.

"North Carolina. It's on the coast."

"This place must seem awfully slow compared with Charlotte."

"You say that like it's a bad thing."

A faint flush of color rose in her cheeks. "I'm sorry, I didn't mean to sound critical. Or at least I shouldn't. Willow Ridge really is a lovely town and the people I've met have been wonderful...for the most part."

"You're not from around here yourself. Your accent is pure Northeast. Boston, maybe?"

"Got it in one. I grew up in Connecticut but went to college in Boston and got into banking there."

"Is it probing if I ask why someone who worked in banking in Boston ended up managing a tiny branch bank in Willow Ridge, Georgia? It's not the back of beyond, but it's close."

The remaining smile and the high color both faded from her face. She hesitated before she said, "Let's just say the reasons were personal and leave it at that."

"All right. I get the feeling there was something very painful behind it, and I'm sorry."

She sighed and tried to find the smile again. "It was painful, but it's in the past. Willow Ridge has given me a new perspective. One I badly needed."

"The town has a lot of virtues," he agreed. "But there are some downsides, too."

"Like everyone knows your business?" she asked. "Or if they don't, they want to?"

He grinned. "Yeah, like that."

"And if you're not married, they want to pair you up with every eligible bachelor in the area."

"That, too." He glanced at her hands. No ring. "I'm presuming you're not married?"

"No. You?"

"Not now. And I've had to tell all the many concerned citizens I don't want to talk about it and I'm not looking for a new relationship."

"I hear you," she said. "Same for me."

"Except, of course, no one believes it."

"There's that. But they have the best possible intentions. They really do want to see you be happy."

"True. And a pain. But actually, when I talked about downsides, I was thinking more along the lines of lack of theaters, museums, concerts, that kind of thing. Shopping options."

A small smile returned to her face. "But it's not that far to drive to Savannah for a lot of those things."

"Good point. Still, the local entertainment options are limited. Unless you're into high school football or baseball games."

"There are little league games, too. The bank is helping to sponsor the local team."

"Good idea," he said. "Lots of local good will."

"I help coach the team, too. I enjoy it." She stared at him for a minute. "You grew up around here. I'll bet you were a star player on the football team. Quarterback?"

"Wide receiver. I was fast but I didn't have the strong arm. And I wasn't a star. That would be Rob Burdeman. He was the quarterback."

"Does he still live here?"

"He works with his dad at Burdeman's Repairs. The most trustworthy place in town to get your car serviced."

"I'll keep that in mind." She sighed. "I may need their services in the near future."

He couldn't help watching and enjoying the changing expressions that shaped her face. Her smile elevated her looks to something way beyond merely pretty. He was attracted, without doubt. But she wasn't available; at least she didn't want to be. That was good news for him, wasn't it?

"Are you planning to stay in Willow Ridge?" he asked.

A spot of color rose in her cheeks. "Probably not. As nice as the place is, I'm more of a city girl. The job here will look good on my resume, though."

Another reason he shouldn't even think about being attracted. Not that he thought he'd stay in Willow Ridge forever, either. But his mother and aunt might need his support for quite a while.

The male half of the cleaning crew leaned in the door to report they were done. Barbara nodded and stood. He drained the soda in his can and collected hers as well, then dumped both into the trash bag on the cleaner's cart just before they rolled it outside to the van. When they had departed, he and Barbara reset the alarms and went out the back door. "Normally I'd be parked back here," she said.

He escorted her around the building to the front. Before she opened the door of her car, she said, "Thank you, Deputy Harper. I appreciate the help. I hope to see you again, but not in this situation."

"Chris," he reminded her. "I'm sure we'll see each other around town. It's inevitable."

She smiled at him, got back in the car, and drove off. He crossed the street in an odd state of bemusement. Her face and figure lingered in his mind. A woman hadn't appealed to him in such a visceral way in a long time. Maybe not since he first met Britt. And if that didn't serve to remind him why getting involved with Barbara Wilton would be a bad idea, then nothing would.

CHAPTER 2

Barbara Wilton tried to concentrate on watching television for a little while, but gave it up as futile. She worked on her notes for the staff meeting before the bank opened in the morning, but she'd already written down everything they needed to cover, including a few developing problems that concerned her. Even throwing in the towel and going to bed didn't wipe him from her mind.

She couldn't get the memory of Deputy Chris Harper out of her head. He had a physical presence out of proportion to his actual size. He was tall, but not overly so, having three or four inches on her own five foot eight, with broad shoulders and lean hips that looked good in the khaki uniform. He might've left football behind a long time ago, but he still moved with the elegant grace and steady control of an athlete.

The lean face was handsome in a comfortable way that put people at ease, though she had a feeling his expression could transform into tough and hard if needed. She didn't want to meet that version of Chris

Harper. But tonight his light blue eyes had sparkled when he laughed, showing adorable dimples in his cheeks. He'd taken off the hat inside, but his light brown hair was just long enough to be stuck down where the rim had sat on it.

In spite of all her vows to avoid getting involved with a man again, the deputy intrigued her. He might've been born and grown up in Willow Ridge, but he'd spent the last few years in Charlotte, and if his comments were any indication, he'd enjoyed some of the cultural advantages of the larger city. Despite the badge, gun, and uniform, he'd managed to put her at ease quickly.

Worse yet, she suspected the attraction was mutual, though he'd made clear he wasn't looking for a relationship any more than she was.

She finally fell asleep but woke feeling less than refreshed the next morning. She had no time to dwell on Deputy Chris, though he tried to invade her thoughts while she showered, dried her hair, and poured coffee into her to-go cup. The day's meetings called for one of her better summer-weight business suits and the Stuart Weitzman beige pumps. The shoes were an indulgence, but after the break-up with Craig, she'd needed something to bolster her spirits and her self-image. She'd borrowed from her savings account last year to get them, and they made her feel good every time she looked down at them on her feet.

Anticipation of the morning meeting and the possibly awkward topics they needed to cover drove Chris Harper from her awareness as she headed to work.

She was the first to arrive. Per protocol, she drove around the building, checking for anything that looked suspicious, then waited in her car in the back parking lot until Tracey Ramirez and Sheila Halloway, her two full-time tellers, pulled in moments later. No one entered the bank alone in the morning.

She got out and went to check inside while the others waited in the car. Once she gave them the all clear sign, the others emerged from the car and entered. The two young women had come together since they lived within a few streets of each other. Better yet, they'd stopped for donuts on the way. Being Boston-born and bred, she'd always considered Dunkin Donuts the last word in that particular confection, but she was quickly becoming a convert to Krispy Kreme's light, hot, fresh-glazed offerings.

Margie Standish, one of her part-timers arrived shortly as well, as polished as usual in a slim navy business suit. Her low-heeled pumps looked new and her purse was definitely Kate Spade. She had a similar one herself. Danny, the other part-timer, had classes in the morning so she'd have to review the material with him later. Last to show up, ten minutes late, was Cindy Martinson, assistant manager and chief thorn in her side.

In her defense Cindy had no doubt expected to be offered the manager's job when it came open, despite her lack of anything beyond a high school GED certificate. She hadn't attempted, much less completed, any of the company-offered training beyond what was absolutely required. Still, it had to be a sore blow when the bank brought in someone from outside. On the other hand, Cindy had declined every opportunity Barbara had offered to learn more on the job and to obtain the necessary credentials to succeed her when she moved on. In fact, the woman made it clear she liked the perks of the title more than she cared for the actual work.

Cindy surveyed the group gathered in the conference room and took a seat at the far end without saying anything.

Barbara took a sip of her coffee. "Now that we're all here. Let's get started. I have several things to go over." The first couple were updates on company policies related to leave time and health insurance. She ran through those quickly. "Next the company has asked me to remind everyone about fraud and scam awareness. Please review the handouts I'm giving you before next week. Each of you will be getting a quiz to complete concerning it. There may be some random testing as well. There are several significant points, but the thing State Branch Bank is concentrating on this week is being aware of emails that look legit and ask you to click on a link to open a document or go someplace on the internet. Be sure you know where those messages are coming from and who sent them before you click on anything in an email. Some of the fake emails can look very realistic. One of these handouts has tips about what to look for."

She looked around the table and sent the stack of handouts around for each to take one.

"Next up, is another reminder to be careful when counting cash or entering check amounts. Some of you already know that you've come up short a couple of times. Accuracy is so important in banking. Our customers expect it from us, as does our employer." Again she surveyed the table trying to keep from singling anyone out. Color rose in Sheila's cheeks. She'd been short twice in the last month, though the amounts were small.

"Last up on my list are a couple more things to be on the lookout for. We've only had this happen once recently, but it could well happen again. Ten days ago we deposited a large check into an individual account that was returned for insufficient funds. The person who made the deposit has no history of receiving large amounts of money, so someone should have looked at it more closely before accepting the check. We fear the person who deposited it was likely the victim of one of those get-rich-quick scams where someone offers you a large sum of money from a Nigerian prince transferring cash. Or possibly someone was told they had won a lottery prize in a contest they didn't know they'd entered. The customer gets a check to deposit but then is expected to pay money back to cover taxes or something like that before they find out the check is no good."

Cindy's eyes narrowed. "They expect us to catch something like that? How are we supposed to recognize that a check is no good? And what do we say to a customer in a case like that?"

"Legitimate questions," Barbara said. And they were, but Cindy's tone made clear her motives were less a request for information and more about a challenge. "But, in fact, we are supposed to notice anything out of the ordinary," she answered. "The bank expects us to pay attention and take note of the unusual. Always look twice at a check for a large amount being deposited in an individual account. Usually, they're legit, but if you see one that looks suspicious, like from a bank overseas or one you've never heard of, or the customer in question has no history or reason that you know of for depositing a large check, bring it to me. Or Cindy. We have a real advantage being a small bank in a small town. We can get to know most of our customers and their situations. And there are protocols for handling questionable situations. The bank is planning to have an online seminar in a couple of weeks to train you in what to say when presented with these situations."

Cindy glared at her but sighed and didn't object further.

Barbara stopped for another sip of coffee. "And here's another one that we need to be aware of. This hasn't happened here yet that I know of, but it could well. If you have a customer wanting to withdraw a large amount of cash, try to gently probe the reasons. Don't interrogate, but you can use a light conversation to try to get at why they're taking out the money. If they tell you anything to indicate that they're being victimized by a scam—you know, like if they say they got a phone call telling them they owe a bunch of back taxes—stall and come get either myself or Cindy. Tell the customer that a withdrawal that large has to be approved by management. You've probably already heard about those kinds of scams where someone gets a call purporting to be from the IRS or where a grandchild is in trouble somewhere. They tend to target the elderly."

"Seems like there's a lot they're expecting us to look out for," Cindy said. "Like we're supposed to be the cops or something."

Barbara suppressed a frustrated sigh. "True. But mostly we're expected to be observant, careful, and aware. People trust us with their money and credit. That's a lot of responsibility and the bank needs its employees to show that it's worthy of the trust."

"Like the job's not hard enough already," Cindy muttered.

"No question that it can be a hard job," Barbara said. "And if anyone finds it too much, then they need to ask themselves if banking is really the right career for them. But there are some perks, too." She put down her notes. "That's it for now. Let's go help some people."

As they were leaving, Sheila said, "Hey, Barbara! I think you met my cousin last night? He's one of the deputies who work with Chris Harper at the sheriff's department. I heard there was a false alarm here."

"There was. And I did meet Deputy Harper. I didn't get the names of the other deputies there. I didn't know one of them was your cousin."

She grinned. "Gary Parker. He's pretty new to the job. That's the thing about Willow Ridge. Everyone knows everyone and we're related to half of them. His grandmother and mine were sisters, which I think makes us second cousins, or something like that. Anyway, if

Cindy seems more disgruntled than usual this morning, it's probably because of that."

"What? Why?"

Sheila looked left and right to be sure no one else was in hearing range. "Cindy's been trying to hook Chris ever since he came back to town, but he's given no sign that he's interested. Then Gary told his mom that Chris looked kind of dazed after he met you. Like he'd gotten hit by a train or something."

"Oh, please. I just met him last night. Word gets around fast."

Sheila grinned. "Haven't you noticed yet? The gossip vine is everywhere, sees everything, hears everything, knows everything. And when you're talking about someone like Chris— smart, good-looking, high-profile job, and single—everyone is interested in what he's doing."

"And that's not a little creepy."

She shrugged. "It is what it is. You've got to admit he's cute, though."

"No question he's attractive. But I'm not in the market."

"Yeah, I don't get that. But whatever." Her expression grew more serious. "Watch out for Cindy. She resents you already. And if Chris takes an interest in you, it's going to get worse. She can be pretty vindictive. Did you ever hear what happened when she thought someone tried to steal her boyfriend in high school? Of course, they never proved it was her—"

The bell pinged, indicating their first customer at the drive-through window. Since that was usually Sheila's station, she sighed and said, "Remind me to tell you about it later."

Barbara didn't want to but nodded. She wouldn't do any prompting, but she had a feeling she'd be hearing the story anyway. The phone rang and she went to answer it.

Right before lunch, Sheila came in with a question about her schedule. Once they had that sorted out, Sheila looked around and then went and closed Barbara's office door before sitting again. She drew a deep breath and huffed it out. "I'm not sure about this… I know you're not one for gossip," she said. "And I get that. Normally I wouldn't tell you something like this, but you should know, if just as a warning. When we were in high school, another girl started flirting with the guy Cindy was dating at the time. I don't know how serious it was on anybody's part, but it doesn't matter. Cindy didn't like it. And…"

She paused and grimaced. "Okay, no one ever proved she did it, but, honestly, we all knew. Anyway, one of the senior girls wore this valuable bracelet that was a family heirloom. She took it off when she washed her hands in the ladies', and when she turned around after drying them, the bracelet had disappeared. It was right after lunch break, so there was a crush of people in there, and no one saw anything. But the next day, Cindy's rival reached into her backpack to pull out a pen and the bracelet fell out. I don't have to tell you what kind of fuss and to-do there was over it. Fortunately for the rival, she could prove she was at band practice at the exact time when the bracelet was stolen. So no one ever got charged with stealing it. We all knew who did it and why. But there was no way to prove it."

Sheila gave her a steady, concerned look. "I mean this like a warning. I don't want to be unfair, and I don't have anything against her personally. Honest. It's just...You need to be careful. She's already unhappy with you getting this job when she thought she should've had it. But if Chris Harper starts paying attention to you, it could be all-out war. And Cindy doesn't play fair. I'm sorry to be saying this, honestly. And maybe it will all be nothing. But you should tread carefully around her." Sheila chewed her lip and wiggled uncomfortably.

Barbara took a moment to consider her response. She generally didn't encourage gossip, but this had a purpose, and Sheila meant well. "Thank you. I appreciate the warning. I already knew Cindy wasn't my biggest fan. I hope she won't do anything that goes that far, but at least I'm now warned about it."

Sheila sighed and her expression relaxed into a smile. "Good. My mission is accomplished then."

They both laughed as she opened the door and left.

The rest of the day proceeded with business as usual. At five Barbara went home to the small house she'd rented. After pouring herself a glass of wine, she settled on the couch for some reading. The Hopeless Romantics Book Club was meeting the next night and she still hadn't gotten to the selected book. She'd picked it up and groaned at the title, "In Love with the Lawman."

It seemed kind of cheesy. Not that she had

any objection to a good romance. In fact, she loved romances. That love had led her to visit Once Upon a Book shortly after she'd moved to town. The bookstore's owner, Edie Rogers, a sweet, petite lady in her early sixties, had sold her a couple of lovely romance novels and convinced her to join the Hopeless Romantics Book Club that met once a month.

Barbara was still grateful for that invitation. Several of the other members were becoming friends, and they understood her reluctance to get involved with another man right now, even if they didn't know all the details. A couple of them had met the men of their dreams recently and were happily planning weddings and honeymoons. She was thrilled for them.

The book proved more engrossing than she anticipated. Lila, the heroine, had buried herself in her work as a physician's assistant ever since the traumatic death of her police officer husband. When Tom, another police detective, enlisted her help in catching a killer working in her hospital, she agreed to assist him but fought against her attraction to him. The last thing she wanted was to fall for another man in a dangerous occupation.

Barbara got so involved in the book it took her stomach growling at quarter to seven to remind her she hadn't had dinner yet. She pulled a boxed meal out of the freezer and put it in the microwave. She read until the machine pinged. Sitting at the table with the tray of hot lasagna and green beans, she propped the book up in front of her.

If the food had any distinctive flavor at all, she missed it, lost in the action where Lila helped save the life of Frank, the detective's best friend. He'd been shot chasing the bad guy who had just tried to commit another murder. Frank survived thanks to the super-human efforts of Lila and a surgeon who treated him right away. Tom was very grateful. He also developed more respect for Lila's medical abilities.

Forcing herself to take a break from the book, Barbara cleaned up after dinner, checked her email and answered a phone message from her mother, reassuring her that life in small-town Georgia was not as primitive as her mom seemed to think. They had a good coffee shop, and upscale shopping was within driving distance.

After preparing for bed, she climbed in with the book, ready to read for a while before falling asleep. She stayed awake as the story wound into its climax where Lila was chased through the hospital by the bad guy while Tom tried to find them both. Fortunately Lila was smart and adept and she managed to trap the villain in a supply closet as Tom closed in. But the villain had one more attack left in him and nearly shot Lila when Tom tried to arrest him. When Tom risked his own life to save her, Lila understood that his job was dangerous, but it also meant helping innocent people and putting away bad ones. They admitted their attraction for each and headed for a happily ever after.

Barbara slept well that night and woke with the memory of a dream that echoed the plot of the book, set in a bank rather than a hospital and with herself as the heroine and Chris Harper as the hero. She refused to indulge that fantasy and pushed it away by creating a mental list of what she needed to do for the day.

The morning passed swiftly with a host of regular tasks—files to be updated, queries answered, reports generated and reviewed, helping out when one of the clerks needed a break and the others were overwhelmed. At lunch she jotted down a few notes about the book for the book club that evening.

Cindy had to leave for a dentist's appointment and a small rush of people needing a banker's help pushed everything else out of her mind. At closing time, she finished up, rushed home to get a quick dinner and change clothes, then headed back into town for thc book club meeting.

CHAPTER 3

Barbara had managed to develop some social life since her arrival in Willow Ridge, if helping to manage a little league team, volunteering for the July Fourth Festival committee, and joining the book club counted as such. Edie, who'd recruited her for the book club, had also talked her into the July Fourth committee, which would have its last meeting the following week. Barbara still had some work to do on her part of the Festival preparation, which involved gathering all the registrations for the parade and the game and food booths. Most were free, but the commercial food operators paid a fee for their spaces. She had her database set up and entries they'd received so far recorded. They still had a day to the deadline, so there was no point doing any more work on it yet.

The other members of the Hopeless Romantics Book Club had begun to gather at the bookstore when she arrived. She found Brooke, a teacher at the local elementary school, and Jayda, a marketing specialist, particularly compatible. She'd occasionally met with a couple of them for coffee at Latte Da, one of the local gathering places and gossip centers in town and the work place of Georgia, another member who'd also been very welcoming.

The early arrivals greeted her with friendly enthusiasm as she made her way to the gathering area in the back. They spent a few minutes catching up and nibbling on snacks before Edie called them to order.

Barbara settled on one end of a comfortable sofa as Edie started by asking each of them for their overall reactions to the story. Most of the women had positive feelings about the book. They agreed it was well-written and engaging. They liked the characters and found the romance realistic.

Some of the women felt that Lila's concern about the danger of the detective's job was overdone and unrealistic, but Barbara disagreed. Having lived the last few years of her life in Boston, reading the paper and listening to television news there, she could sympathize. Too many law enforcement officers had died or been seriously injured in the line of duty.

"But that's like living in fear," one of the others said. "It's not a good way to live your life."

"Very true," Barbara agreed. "But sometimes after something bad has happened, it's hard to avoid being fearful."

"But do you want to let it cripple your life though?" Edie asked. "You could be missing out on so much." Edie had last her own husband a few years back so they all knew she understood the pain.

"The part that really got me," Sorcha said, "was when he asked her, 'Was it worth it? Would you give up the five good years you had with him to avoid the pain of his loss?' I thought that was powerful."

"It's a good question, too," Bronte added. "Do the memories of happiness outweigh the pain of loss?"

"But loss isn't guaranteed," Sorcha responded. "At least not immediate loss. I don't think it's the same kind of measurement after, say, thirty years."

"Nothing in life is guaranteed."

"And you're not really living if you spend all your time isolated in a cocoon to avoid pain."

Barbara considered all of the points people had made. "Is there a time limit or balance involved? I mean is it worth the pain of loss if you only had a year together? Or six months, or even a few weeks? Or say, if you had to go through the pain of loss twice in a short period of time? Wouldn't you try harder to avoid being in that situation again?"

Edie and a couple of the others present regarded her thoughtfully. Barbara suspected they sensed the question wasn't just rhetorical but came from personal experience.

"All trauma leaves wounds," Edie said. "But wounds heal. They may leave scars, but those don't—or shouldn't—impede functioning. Still, healing takes time, and everyone recovers differently. There are a lot of factors that impact how quickly or slowly one heals."

Barbara felt both comforted and encouraged by those words. She didn't say anything more about trauma, and the discussion turned to some of the secondary characters in the book and then to the plot structure. She offered her own views occasionally, but none of those touched her in the same personal way.

After a couple of hours, the meeting broke up and they all headed out. But when Barbara got to her car and turned the key, the only response was a few clicks and a grinding noise that didn't get the motor started. She tried a couple more times, growing more and more frustrated and upset, but the Lexus refused to start.

She pulled out her cell phone before she realized she had no idea who to call. She'd never signed up for Triple-A, and the service stations would be closed this time of night. All of the other ladies had departed, so there wasn't anyone around to ask for a jump.

Fortunately a light still shone in the book store, so Edie was likely still there. Barbara got out and crossed the street to tap on the door. Edie appeared after a few moments and invited her in. "Problem?" she asked as she led the way to the lounge in back.

"My car won't start. I think the battery's dead. Can I leave it parked out front? I'll get an Uber home and get someone to tow it in the morning."

Edie laughed. "Honey, you're not in Boston anymore. The only Uber driver we have in town is Sam Comerford, and trust me, you don't want to get into a car with him. Give me a minute."

The woman went to the phone at the desk and pressed a number. After identifying herself and explaining the problem she listened for a minute and said "Thank you," before hanging up.

"Help is on the way," she told Barbara. "It will take a few minutes. I usually have some hot chocolate before bed. Would you join me?"

"That sounds great," Barbara said. "Even though it's still like eighty-five out there."

"Late June in Georgia isn't always pleasant," Edie agreed. "But these days we all have air conditioning and wonder how we ever got anything done in summer without it." She used a hot plate to warm milk and pulled packets of chocolate mix out of a cabinet. "May I ask you a personal question?" she said, while stirring the cocoa powder into the milk.

Barbara suspected she knew what she wanted to ask and realized she might be able to talk about it with this woman. "Go ahead."

"I have the feeling you were speaking from personal experience when you talked about the effects of trauma on people."

She didn't couch it as a question, but the inquiry was there.

"You're right." Barbara had to clear her throat to get rid of the sudden obstruction there. "I was engaged twice in four years."

Edie turned around to look at her. "But you're not married now so something bad happened both times."

"I was engaged to Gavin for almost two years. He was killed in a traffic accident a month before the wedding. That was... I can't even describe how horrible it was. It took me a couple of years before I started dating again. I met Craig and fell in love again. We got engaged, but after a few months, he broke up with me. He'd met someone else and his feelings for her were stronger than his love for me. I let him go with minimal raging and tears. But it broke something inside of me. Something that had survived Gavin's death. Maybe it was just my pride, but I felt drained and empty. That was when I decided I needed a completely new start, somewhere very different from Boston. I was on a management career path and needed experience as a branch manager, so when this job came open, I jumped on it. I liked that it took me out of Boston, to a pretty much completely different world."

"I'm so sorry, my dear." Edie handed her a cup of hot chocolate. "That is more tragedy and pain than anyone should have to endure. You have incredible strength and resilience. I can't imagine how difficult it was to pull up roots and move to some place so different and start over."

"Thanks. Moving here has helped a lot. I needed to get away from a place where everyone knew of my 'bad luck' and constantly gave me pitying glances and condescending tolerance. Even my family... Of course they mean well and want me to be happy, but they were all trying so hard to make me feel better, and that wasn't what I needed."

"No, I wouldn't think so."

"I haven't told anyone but you about my past, and I hope you'll keep it to yourself. Let everyone think I'm eccentric or a wacky Yankee if needed. Almost everyone's been very nice and accepting here and I've enjoyed it. Of course, there are a few who may not be as thrilled, but I can live with it. I've—"

A tap on the door interrupted her. Edie put

down her cup and went to answer.

Barbara recognized the voice at the door. She should've guessed who Edie would call for help.

She stood up, set aside the nearly empty cup of hot chocolate, and walked to the door. "Hi, Chris," she said as she approached.

He looked from Edie to her and smiled, flashing that gorgeous set of dimples and lighting up his blue eyes. "Hey, Barbara. I hear you have a problem?"

She nodded. "Car won't start. I think it's the battery."

"How old is it?"

"The car? About six years."

"I meant the battery."

"Oh. It's the original that came with the car."

"It doesn't owe you anything then," he said. "Anyway, I parked right in front of your car, and I have jumper cables. Let's see what we can do." He led the way across the street. He'd parked his car so the front faced the front of hers.

He went to the trunk of the official car he drove and pulled out the jumper cables. Once they had the front hoods of both vehicles open, he hooked up the cables and told her to try starting the Lexus. It coughed, then roared to life.

Edie stood nearby, watching, so Barbara called her thanks to her. The woman waved and went back inside. Chris Harper tapped on her window, and she lowered it, allowing a wave of hot, humid air into the vehicle.

He leaned in to say, "That battery's likely shot. If you want to take your car directly to the service center and leave it there, I'll give you a lift home. They have a night box you can drop the keys in. Or you can drive it home, and if it doesn't start in the morning, call for a tow."

He waited while she thought it over. "I guess it'll save me the cost of a tow to take it to the service center tonight."

"Good choice. Follow me."

He got back in the official car and started it, turned it around in the road, and waited for her to get behind him. The service center was a little over a mile away, so it didn't take long to get there. Chris pointed to where she should leave the car and then waited while she put the keys in the locked box.

She sat in his vehicle with him, told him where she lived, and spent a few minutes marveling at all the switches and gadgets on the dashboard and between the seats. "I've never been in a sheriff's car before. You have a lot of equipment in here."

"Helps us do the job."

A radio crackled with brief exchanges of words that she mostly didn't understand. "Are they speaking English? I thought I heard an 'in progress' in there but the rest of it didn't make much sense."

"Ten codes. A lot of departments are abandoning them in favor of plain English, but we still use them. The one Brian said meant a traffic stop in progress. The other was an acknowledgement by dispatch that he was occupied."

"I see. This place must seem slow compared to Charlotte. I mean, how many Charlotte cops have time to jump-start a car and then take the driver to a service center and back home again?"

"Not many," he admitted. "I certainly didn't. But actually I don't mind the slower pace. There's still plenty to keep me busy. And even though Willow Ridge may seem peaceful, we get our share of calls for domestic disputes, robberies in progress, fugitives in the area, things like that. With such a small department, we have times when we get really busy. Fortunately tonight's not one of those times."

"It's too hot for most people to have the energy to commit a crime."

He smiled. "There's that. But the heat does tend to provoke more arguments. A lot of people have short fuses in the summer around here."

"Hadn't considered that. I suppose it makes sense. I've noticed that some parents can be argumentative at the little league games I've been to. A couple of times I've worried we'd have to call your department."

"I forgot you help to coach a little league team. How did that happen?" he asked.

"I've always been a baseball fan. I played in little league growing up and liked it. Even played softball in college. When Edie found out she told me one of the local teams needed help. I got a phone call from the dad who functioned as a coach a couple of days later, begging me to assist. We tried it out one Saturday a couple of months ago, and it went pretty well. Their players—especially the pitchers—needed help and the dad admitted he didn't know anything about it."

"You were a pitcher?"

"I had a mean curveball in eighth grade. But I switched to playing outfield in college.

Pitching softball is different from baseball, and I wasn't as good at it."

"And after that?"

"There is no after that. I blew out my knee sliding into first my senior year in college, and that ended it. There's nowhere for women to go anyway."

She couldn't see his expression in the darkness, but she heard it in his voice. "Were you safe?"

"At first? Yes."

"Worth it?"

"In the big picture? Probably not. But at the time. Yes. My team went to the division championships."

"Too bad you couldn't play," he said.

"We might've won it if I had been playing. Lost by one run. But it was a great experience."

"I still play some baseball, too. Not regularly, though. I might have to drop by one of your games."

"That would be great. I hope we don't need you to separate angry parents."

"I hope not, too."

He pulled into the driveway of her rented house. Before she got out, he said, "What time do you usually leave for work?"

"Most days about eight. The bank opens at nine."

"How about if I pick you up tomorrow morning and take you there?"

She opened the door, hoping the interior light would come on so she could see his face. The car did light up, but his carefully blank expression didn't tell her much. "You don't have to do that. You've already gone above and beyond in bringing me home."

"I know I don't have to. It would be my pleasure to do it, though."

She hesitated, wanting to have time to think about it. She felt like more rode on the question than just a lift to work. But she couldn't leave him hanging. "Okay. Thank you."

CHAPTER 4

He got her phone number and said he'd text her in the morning when he arrived at her house. Chris drove back to the office, wondering what crazy impulse had moved him to offer the ride to work. Not that he was regretting it. Not exactly.

He went inside the sheriff's office just long enough to submit some paperwork and clock out, then hopped into his pickup truck to head home. Home being his mother's house. Not for the first time he wondered how bad it looked to others for a thirty-two-year-old man to be living with his mother.

But the arrangement was practical, given his mom's failing health and his own lack of assets. He'd offered his ex-wife the house, with its thirty thousand in equity and two hundred grand mortgage along with most of the furniture, in lieu of alimony. He kept his battered old pickup. She got the new Mercedes he never drove anyway. At least they had no kids to be wrecked by the break-up. They'd both wanted a family but thought it better to wait a while. He wondered now if they'd each sensed early on that the marriage was a mistake.

His mother had already gone to bed by the time he returned home, but she'd left a casserole in the refrigerator in case he was hungry. He wasn't especially, but his mom would be concerned if he didn't eat something, so he took a bit and warmed it in the microwave.

At his request, his mom kept a running list of things around the house that needed fixing or replacing. She posted it on the refrigerator. He checked the page, considering which ones he'd tackle tomorrow on his day off.

He rose as usual around seven to the smell of coffee and bacon, showered, and dressed in jeans and a polo shirt. His mom stood at the stove frying eggs. He couldn't help but notice that she'd lost more weight and looked thinner and frailer. But when she turned to greet him, her smile was bright, and she sat down at the table after she'd set out plates of food for each of them. She'd given herself smaller portions, but she ate it all.

"Where are you off to this morning?" she asked.

"Got a couple of errands to run," he answered. "Promised to drop someone off at work and then I thought I'd head to the hardware store and pick up a new light and fixtures for the upstairs bathroom. It's going to be too hot to work outside today."

"True. The person you're dropping off at work... Is it that pretty new bank manager?"

He looked up sharply. "What makes you

think that?"

"Heard that the battery in her car died after Edie's book club last night and you jumped it for her. But that wouldn't fix it, so I figured she'd need some help again this morning."

He shook his head. "I should've known it would be all over town this morning."

"Are you interested in her? I hear she's attractive. But she's a Yankee, so I don't know if it's a good idea."

He forced a laugh. "Mom, I thought we put those North and South differences to bed a while back. Like more than a hundred years ago."

"Well, yes, but... They're still different. And especially if shc's from one of those big cities."

"Boston. She moved here from Boston. But she likes Willow Ridge. And I don't know why we're even discussing this. I met her less than a week ago, in the line of duty."

His mother studied him and raised an eyebrow. "You're driving her to work this morning. And I'm pretty sure that isn't anywhere in your job description."

He hated the color he felt rising in his face. "I'm just being neighborly. Showing her some of the advantages of living in a small town. We look out for each other here."

"Okay." His mom stood and picked up her plate. "Try to find bathroom taps with a finish that won't show all the water and soap marks."

"Got it."

"Oh, and Ruth asked if you could take a look at her washing machine. It's making strange noises."

"That's not good. I'll go by there after I fix the

bathroom," he promised.

He rinsed his dishes and put them in the dishwasher, knowing full well his mom would pull them out and hand wash them after he left.

When he reached Barbara's driveway, he stopped and pulled out the phone to text her, but she appeared at the door before he could press the send button, so she must've been watching for him. She locked the house behind her. Despite the predicted heat she wore a light-weight business suit with a long-sleeved jacket. Her shoes had medium high heels. Of course the bank had air conditioning. She looked even more elegant and classy than the previous two times he'd seen her. In Boston she likely fit right in, but that level of sophistication stood out in Willow Ridge. He hopped out to get the passenger door for her.

She looked him up and down and smiled. "You look different out of uniform. More approachable."

"Less authority figure, more guy next door?" he suggested.

"Something like that. You're off today?"

She got in and he went around to the driver's side. He started the motor before answering. "They let me have the occasional day off."

"Are you going fishing or hunting? Isn't that what most of the men around here do on their days off?"

"Stereotype alert. Not all Southern males spend all their time fishing or hunting—though to be fair, they are pretty common hobbies. But actually I'm going to work on some upgrades to a bathroom in my mom's house and stop by my Aunt Ruth's place later. Her washing machine is making funny noises."

"Oh dear. That's a problem," she said.

"Right. Although with Aunt Ruth, there's no telling what it might mean. She's getting a bit...forgetful. We've been trying to convince her to move in with Mom, but she's lived in that house for sixty-some years. It's the big white one on the corner of Seventh and Cherry Street."

"I've seen it. It's a beauty, but it looks like a lot of house for one person."

"She and my Uncle Sherm used to take in boarders and occasionally fostered kids who needed a home before he died, but she's too old for that now. Still, they fixed it up for a disabled person when Uncle Sherm got sick."

"That's tough."

"It is. But enough of my family drama. What does your day look like?" He realized too late that in asking that, it might sound like he was angling for a date.

"Work until five, then get home, eat, and head to the park for practice with the team."

"What age group have you got?"

"Tens and Elevens. Good age. They mostly haven't developed any bad habits yet. Or bad attitudes."

"But plenty of energy and enthusiasm."

"That's the truth. I don't know how they do it in this heat, but it doesn't seem to stop them, even when I'm sitting in the shade with a pocket fan on myself."

At her direction, he drove around to the back of the bank building. One of the tellers, Margie Something, was already there, waiting in her car.

"Do you need a ride after work?" he asked Barbara.

"Thanks, but I don't think so. I'll have a co-worker drop me off at the service center. I do appreciate your taking the time to do this, though."

"My pleasure. Have a good day."

Her smile and the lovely, flowery aroma—some kind of perfume, he supposed—that surrounded her were working on him, making his heartbeat speed up and blood rush. He wanted to lean over and kiss her, but he restrained the impulse. That he had it, though, was both exciting and disturbing.

Even after she'd gotten out and waved as she went inside the bank, the image of her face and body stayed in his mind while he drove to the big box hardware store up the highway. Ordinarily he'd go to the small, locally-owned shop downtown, but they didn't carry some of the things he needed for this project.

When he found himself wandering along the aisles of the huge store instead of heading right to the section he needed, he lectured himself about getting his head back in the game and paying attention to what he was doing. With an effort of will, he moved Barbara Wilton to the back of his mind.

He found what he needed and drove back, using the time to work out the order of the tasks for the upgrade. The bathroom project took all of the morning and all of his attention. Fortunately his Mom had left a note saying she was going shopping, which meant she'd likely be out for most of the day, since 'shopping' seemed to cover a lot of ground, including coffee with friends at Latte Da, checking out the latest arrivals at several clothing, book, and gift stores, as well as catching up on all the gossip. He winced when he thought about how much of that gossip would be about him.

But the upgrade demanded all his attention for the next few hours. The results looked even better than he hoped when he finally finished and cleaned up. Mom would be pleased.

He fixed himself a sandwich for a late lunch then headed for Aunt Ruth's place. She greeted him with her usual hugs and enthusiasm, but he winced a little when she called him "Ron," his father's name.

"I'm Chris, Aunt Ruth," he reminded her. "Ron's son."

"Oh, right, of course. I'm sorry. You look so much like him."

He'd seen pictures of his dad at the age he was now and there was a definite resemblance.

"Have you had lunch yet?" Aunt Ruth asked.

"Yes, ma'am." He glanced around and noticed some pictures hanging askew and places where the paint was chipping. He could straighten the frames, but the paint was for another time. "Mom said you were having some trouble with your clothes washer?"

"Oh, yes, it was making some loud thunkety-thunk noises."

"When it was spinning or rinsing?"

She gave him a blank look. "No idea."

"Okay, let's try it out. Do you have some towels or sheets that need washing?"

She disappeared and reappeared shortly with an armload of towels. He put them in the machine, a fairly new top-loader, added detergent, and started it. The machine sounded normal as the tub filled with water.

"It doesn't usually do it at the beginning. It's more when it's pushing the water out," she said.

He began to have a suspicion about the problem, but it wouldn't show up until it went into the spin cycle. While they waited, he asked if he could fix the pictures that weren't hanging straight and one where the frame had cracked. She found some basic tools and he set to work while keeping an ear on the washing machine's progress.

Aunt Ruth kept up a steady stream of conversation, filling him in on all the news and gossip about all her friends in town. Except that some of the people cited had passed on years ago and several bits of "news" had occurred quite a while in the past. She called him Ron more than once.

The washing machine switched into its first spin cycle and he went to listen. It sounded normal. Aunt Ruth followed and they waited through another rinse and into a second spin. No noises happened. To confirm his hunch, he lifted the lid and rearranged the towels, moving them all to one side. When he restarted it, the unbalanced load did make a loud thunking and shook the machine.

"Is that what it sounds like?" he asked.

"Yes, that's it!"

He swallowed a sigh and said, "Okay, I know how to fix it. Can you get me the hammer and pliers, a piece of paper, some tape and a marker?" he asked.

While she went to collect the items, he tried

to decide where to post the sign and how best to do it so she'd remember. Once she returned, he asked her to get him a beer. While she was gone, he tapped around with the hammer to make her think he was doing something, then lettered and illustrated a sign showing how to distribute towels in the machine, which he posted on the wall nearby.

"I've got it fixed," he told her when she returned with the beer. After a long drink he continued, "But to prevent future problems you need to be sure to load heavy things like towels evenly in the bottom." He showed her the wet towels in the machine before he pulled them out and transferred them to the drier.

Aunt Ruth nodded and thanked him for fixing it.

Hearing the mail carrier at the door, she went to collect the mail while he finished his drink. She came back walking slowly, staring at a letter in her hand. She looked up and saw him.

"Ron? What is this? I think it says I haven't paid the mortgage and they're going to foreclose on the house. Can that be right? Do I have a mortgage?"

He muttered a few words under his breath, words Aunt Ruth wouldn't approve of if she heard them. Louder, he said, "Yes, you have a mortgage. Uncle Sherm refinanced the house ten years ago to pay for the kitchen and bathroom renovations. Let me see that."

CHAPTER 5

Barbara's day had started off well with the lift from Chris Harper, but it went downhill after that. Sheila was out sick with a summer cold, so Barbara sometimes had to help the tellers out during busy times. Cindy should have been doing that, but she said she had another appointment and left at ten. She didn't return until almost two. Being down two people meant Barbara neglected most of her own work to assist when the lines grew long. Some of the customers wanted to chat and she hated to be rude to anyone.

She had only a few minutes here and there to replay in her mind just how good Chris Harper had looked in the casual jeans and polo shirt. Not that he didn't look great in uniform, too, but out of it, he looked more like a man who would be fun to spend time with. The change in him went beyond the clothes, though. Off duty he was less intense, less stern, more...well, as she'd told him earlier, more approachable. Even more attractive.

She berated herself for how much she

wanted to approach him. That would be foolish, though. In uniform or out, he didn't seem like a man who wanted to do light, casual relationships. And she wasn't sure she was willing to risk even that much after the hard lessons life had taught her. Besides, as much as she liked the place, she didn't plan to spend the rest of her life in Willow Ridge. She had a career to build and the experience here would serve her well, but moving up in the banking industry meant going to a larger city, like back to Boston or onto Atlanta or Charlotte.

Barbara was in the midst of sorting out some paperwork that afternoon when one of the tellers called her to the front desk.

"Look at this." Danny, the part-time afternoon clerk, showed her an image of a cancelled check on his computer screen.

She stared at it but didn't see anything unusual. Written on the account of Mr. and Mrs. J. Kingston Percy to a landscaping company for a hundred and seventy dollars. "What about it?"

"This is Mrs. Percy," Danny said, nodding to the customer standing at the counter. "And she didn't write this check."

"It's signed by Mr. Percy." Barbara looked at the woman. "You've asked your husband about this?"

The woman, who appeared to be about fifty, was impeccably groomed and dressed. "My husband has Parkinson's," she answered. "He hasn't signed a check himself in years. Also, if you look at the check, it's numerically way out of order. I don't even have checks with those numbers."

Danny showed the transaction list from her account. The most recent checks processed had numbers between four thousand and five thousand. This one was seven thousand four hundred and twenty.

"Potential identity theft. Go ahead to the next customer," she told Danny. "I'll take care of this." She looked at Mrs. Percy and said, "Come with me, please, and I'll see if we can get this squared away." She kept a smile on her face. Her sigh was entirely inward. Identity theft was messy and involved a lot of paperwork.

Once in her office, she asked Mrs. Percy for the information she needed to look up the account. A quick check through their history turned up no red flags that might indicate someone attempting to scam the bank. She pulled up the scanned image of the out-of-order check and compared it with scanned images of other checks the woman had written. The handwriting and signature were consistent on all the lower-numbered checks. The one in question looked decidedly different. But... She squinted at the scan. The style of the check itself was the same as the others.

After typing a bit more, she turned to Mrs. Percy. "I've put a stop payment on the checks in the seven thousand range and refunded the amount of this one to your account. We'll have to file a report with the sheriff's department. Now, I have a few questions I have to ask for paperwork for the bank. Please don't be insulted. I'm not implying you or anyone in your family was responsible. We just have to cover the bases for reporting this. Since the check is in the same style as your other checks, did you look at all of the blank checks you have to be sure none are missing? And do you know what the last number of your current batch of checks is?"

Mrs. Percy had already done a lot of the background work for her. She'd carefully leafed through the books of blank checks she had at home to make sure all were there. And the highest number she had was four thousand nine hundred. She kept the checks locked in her desk drawer. Her adult children and grandchildren were in and out of the house, and the adults knew where she kept them, but the handwriting on the bad check didn't resemble that of any of her children. She had heard of the landscape service it was written to but had never done business with them.

An hour later they finished with the paperwork, including her helping Mrs. Percy to file an online report with the sheriff's department. Cindy had arrived and overheard part of the conversation as they filled out the forms. "What's up with her?" Cindy asked as Mrs. Percy finally departed.

Barbara explained about the fraudulent check. "Are you sure her husband didn't write it and forget to tell her about it?"

"She said it's not her husband's handwriting. He doesn't sign anything anymore since he has Parkinson's. And the check number isn't even in their current check batch."

Cindy shrugged. "I heard he was a bit around the bend."

Barbara bristled at the callousness of that remark but didn't address it other than to say,

"That may be so, but the evidence still points to someone else having written the check. There may be more of them out there yet, too. And even if we doubt the customer, good service means we start by—" She stopped when she noticed Cindy wasn't paying attention.

A man had come through the front door and stopped right inside. Because he was silhouetted against the light, it her a moment to recognize Chris Harper. He turned, saw them standing near her office, and started toward them.

"That was fast," she said, smiling at him. "I just filed the report fifteen minutes ago…"

Her smile faded as she took in his expression and the storm clouds brewing in the tightly drawn brows and narrowed eyes. He wasn't in uniform or even on duty. But he was definitely upset about something.

"What's up?" she asked.

He held a paper out toward her. "This." The word wasn't loud but held a load of pent-up anger. "What's going on? And why didn't you warn me?"

"About what?" She took the paper from him and did a quick scan. "Oh, no."

"What is it?" Cindy asked, staring from one of them to the other.

"A demand for payment letter," Barbara answered. "It's the last step before foreclosure. On a house here in Willow Ridge."

"My Aunt Ruth's," Chris said. "Why didn't you say anything about it yesterday? You must've known."

"No, I didn't. Why would I know about it?"

"She and Uncle Sherm got the original

mortgage here from your bank and refinanced it here ten years ago. How could you not know? In fact, did you do this?" His tone grew softer and even angrier.

Cindy, watching them both avidly, said, "Ruth Freeman's house? That beautiful Victorian? They're going to foreclose on it?"

Barbara gave her a sharp look. "This is private bank business. Do not say a word about it outside this office." She turned back to Chris. "I didn't do it. I didn't know about it. Look at the name of the bank on the letter."

"Regional Banking. So?"

"This isn't Regional Banking. It's a branch of State Branch Bank of Georgia."

"What's the difference? I know she refinanced the mortgage through this bank branch."

Barbara stared at the paper again before meeting his angry gaze. "Like many banks we process mortgage applications, but we don't service them. They're sold to larger banks that handle mortgages. Once we pass it off to them, what happens is out of our hands."

"What kind of idiocy is that?" he asked, unmollified. "Your bank advertises itself as being a local bank serving the local community."

"I know, but servicing mortgages is complicated and time consuming. It's a common practice for small banks to sell them to another bank after the initial processing."

He took the letter back from her. "So, our local community bank can't help us when we have a crisis."

This was a version of Chris Harper she

hadn't wanted to see. Eyes narrowed and mouth firmly clenched, anger radiated from him. He didn't quite look menacing, but intimidating... Yes.

She drew in a breath and let it out on a sigh. "I didn't say that. I'm trying to explain why I didn't know anything about this. Heck, even if I had known about it, I couldn't tell you anything. I'd be violating privacy laws. But I had no clue. And the bank per se can't do much to help, but maybe I can, as an individual." She looked around, noting that several customers had turned to watch them. Hopefully they were far enough way that they couldn't hear the actual words exchanged. "Why don't you come in and sit down?"

He tipped his head and followed her into her office. Cindy appeared inclined to follow but Barbara nodded toward the lines forming at the teller counter and shut the door after Chris had entered.

"First of all," she asked. "Why did you wait until now to do something about this?"

He remained very still, his expression fixed. "This is the first I've heard about it."

"Your Aunt Ruth should have gotten multiple notices. The banks generally give you plenty of warning before going to foreclosure."

"She didn't say anything about it." He sighed and his stiff posture relaxed slightly. "Aunt Ruth is starting to have some problems...with memory and organization. When this showed up this morning, she acted like she had no idea there were any issues with the mortgage. I guess I assumed someone here at this bank would let us know before anything like this happened."

"But she must've missed several payments. There would've been other notices. By mail and likely by phone. The demand letter is the last effort before foreclosure. You still have time to act but not much."

"What do we have to do?" There were still hints of anger in his tone, but the initial fury seemed to have lessened.

"Call the number on the demand letter and explain that you want to settle the account. They might even be willing to let you make a partial payment, but they may not. You might have to pay off all the back payments plus penalties. Can your family do that?"

"Honestly? I don't know. If I read that right, it's almost ten thousand dollars."

Barbara took the paper back and glanced through it. "You're right about the amount. Here's another question to ask the family. What are you going to do about the house if you can save it from foreclosure? And what are you going to do about your aunt? If she's already missed payments on the mortgage, the odds aren't good that she'll start paying regularly now. And you really should look into other things—like the utilities. She may well be in arrears on those, too."

His expression changed, looking stricken now. "I hadn't even thought of that."

Her heart hurt for him. This was a shock, but it also presented a significant family problem that went deeper than finances. And it had to be humiliating as well. Not that she'd let him see anything beyond a professional, surface sympathy. Bad enough she had to give him this terrible news.

After a moment or two of withdrawn silence, he shook himself out of it and picked up the letter from her desk. "I'll need to talk to my Mom and maybe a cousin or two about this." He stood. "Thank you for the advice." He sounded sincere in the gratitude, but the words lacked the personal warmth of their earlier interactions.

Barbara stood as well and walked out with him. He gave a quick nod as he hurried out the door and across the sidewalk to his truck. She was all too aware that everyone in the bank watched as she returned to her office.

Trying to get back to her regular work was futile. Concentration on anything but Chris's problems and his distress proved impossible for the last half hour of the day.

Once they'd closed up, Danny gave her a lift to the service center to get her car, then she headed home for a quick supper before little league practice that evening.

Ever since she was a kid she'd enjoyed playing baseball. If she no longer had a way to play it herself, at least coaching and teaching children the game provided an outlet for her interest. She still had her own pair of cleats.

Barbara spent most of the practice time that evening working with the young pitchers, reinforcing her previous lessons on how to hold the ball, balance, align their stances, and raise the ball to throw. She'd taken an online course the previous year in how to teach kids to pitch without risking damage to their developing bodies. These youngsters were just beginning to learn the basics, so she kept it simple.

Most of them tried to imitate the stance and motions of big-league pitchers they'd seen on television, which wasn't all bad, but they had no grasp of why those men did what they did. She had to explain over and over that they needed to understand and practice the fundamentals before they could work on the subtle adjustments that professionals made.

She took heart each time one of them managed to throw a strike. In the month she'd been working with them, she'd seen a significant increase in the number of pitches that hit the zone.

And though she didn't try to flaunt it, she enjoyed discovering that she could still get balls over the plate consistently herself, with the asterisk that the distance from the mound to the plate was less than in regular baseball.

When one of the men who'd been watching from the stands approached her after practice, she braced herself for a possible confrontation with a parent who didn't like her advice to his kid. But that wasn't what happened. "I been watching you and I got something to ask," he said. "Walker Ave. Baptist has a team that plays in a tri-county league. Right now we're down a couple of people and we could use some help. Would you consider it?"

"Playing or coaching?"

"Some of both, but mostly playing."

"Me?" she asked. "Isn't it a men's league?"

"Well, yeah, mostly, but there ain't no rule says it has to be. And some of the other teams do have women playing. Thing is, I've watched you and I'm betting you hit better 'n all but a couple of the guys on the team."

"I'm hitting pitches from eleven-year-olds. Of course, it looks good."

"Yeah, but you got the form and the eye. And you maybe pitch better most of our guys, too."

"Again, little league distance."

"As may be," he said, "But I sure wish you'd at least come try it out. Truth is, we aren't very good. And there's only about a month left in the season, so there's no big pressure to win now. You'd be doing us a big favor."

"What times are we talking about?"

He told her what nights they practiced and played and the weekend times. Those did fit into her schedule, so she agreed to show up for the next practice on Saturday morning.

"What positions do you need help with?"

"Second base and maybe sometimes pitching," he told her.

She waved goodbye to the players as they left, then drove home, hoping she wasn't getting in over her head. She hadn't played a real game in a long time.

Once she returned home she put her concerns over playing baseball aside and spent some time getting the registrations for the Festival completed with the money ready to turn over to the treasurer. Most of the registrations had come via the form on the website, so she logged in and downloaded them to a flash drive she devoted to the Festival. After printing them out, she matched up each form with the credit card payments. Only one hadn't been paid that way.

She collected the envelopes that had been mailed in and opened each. Four of the five held checks along with forms, including one that covered the online form that wasn't paid by credit card. The fifth held a pile of bills, mostly tens and fives, folded up in a piece of white paper. They added up to the correct amount and she attached the stack of cash to the registration from with a binder clamp. The rest of the checks were paper-clipped to the forms, and she noted all of them in the database she'd set up.

By ten o'clock everything was in order and she headed for bed, exhausted.

The next morning it occurred to her the treasurer for the Festival Committee, the person she'd be turning the money over to, was Cindy. That gave her pause, in light of Sheila's warning. But since she had no choice about transferring it, she opted to take pictures of the forms with money or checks attached before she left for work.

When she got there, she had Tracey watch her count the cash she'd brought and sign a paper as witness that Barbara had carried in the cash and locked it in her desk. Cindy was late getting in that morning.

Friday remained an average day up until eleven when Chris Harper came to her office again. Because she was deeply involved in studying a report on the screen, she didn't see him enter and jumped a bit when he tapped on the open door.

"Sorry to startle you. I'm following up on the report you filed about a bad check yesterday."

"Oh right. Come in." She waved him to a chair.

He was in uniform, and his expression made clear this was purely a professional visit. That didn't stop her breath from getting a bit tight and her pulse speeding up. Even with that steely look, he was still very attractive.

"Can you show me the check in question?" he asked.

"Mrs. Percy has requested the original from the central office, but I've printed an image of it." She handed him the copy.

He opened the file folder he held. "I've talked to Della Percy, who swears she didn't write this check. I've got handwriting samples from her, her husband, and one of her adult children. I'm waiting for the other to return from a business trip, but I did see a note he'd left her, and it doesn't look too similar. None of their writing even remotely matches the check."

"I've looked at a number of checks she's written in the past. The handwriting was consistent and looked nothing like this."

He showed her the other writing samples. A quick glance sufficed to confirm they didn't match.

"I also had her show me her check supply," he said. "There aren't any that are near this number."

"I know." She turned to the computer. "I'm looking for the check order." She had to scroll through a list. "And here it is. That's odd. It should've been flagged as suspicious. An order was submitted ten weeks ago for a small batch of checks that include the number on that fraudulent check. And it was sent to a different address. How many red flags do you need? But apparently no one noticed anything out of the ordinary. If any live person ever looked at it at all." She told the computer to print out the order, went and got the sheet from the printer, and handed it to him.

"The shipping address isn't the Percys'," he said.

"I know. Hold on a minute. Let me see where that is."

She brought up a maps app on her computer and put in the address on the order. Before she could turn the screen so he could see it, he'd stood and come around to look over her shoulder, which put him close enough for her to sense the warmth of his body. She pushed down the fine tremble that worked its way through her and made an effort to keep her fingers steady on the mouse as she manipulated it.

"Right here." She moved the cursor in a circle around the house. "That's not even close to where the Percys live."

"No." He moved back to the chair. "I'll check at that place next. Meanwhile, how hard is it to order checks like that? Wouldn't they need to have the Percys' account number?"

"Yes, they would." She went back to looking at the check order. "There's no indication whether this was submitted via the internet or mail. I can do some digging to find that out, but I'm not sure it matters. The point is it looks like someone got hold of their account number and is using it. I suppose in theory anyone they wrote a check to would have the necessary information."

"Aren't most orders submitted online these days?" he asked.

"Most. Not all. A lot of older people aren't comfortable with the technology. Usually they'll come to the bank and ask us to submit the order for them. Or mail in one of those renewal slips that comes packaged with the checks."

"How common is this kind of thing? I didn't do anything with the Fraud unit in Charlotte. As far as I know this is the first time it's happened here."

"Identity theft is more common than most people know. I saw it happen several times in Boston."

"Wouldn't have thought it could happen here, though," he said. "But banking is getting so impersonal and computerized that no one knows anything anymore." The last words were laced with a subtle bitterness.

"And law enforcement isn't getting more computerized? And nothing ever gets lost in the shuffle?"

He gave her a hard stare before his expression relaxed. "Point taken. But I need to get back to work. Some old-fashioned detective work."

"What are you going to do?"

"Talk to the people at that address." He pointed to the copy of the order. "I also need to visit the garden center that deposited the check. See if they can figure out who gave it to them."

"Sounds like a plan," she said.

She stood when he did, but before he turned to go, he looked at her for a moment. His eyes narrowed and lips twitched as though he wanted to say something but wasn't sure he should. Finally, he just shook his head, picked up his hat, and said, "Thank you for your time," as he walked out.

Right before quitting time, Barbara got out the forms and payments to give to Cindy. She tried to make sure several people were around to witness that she did hand the stack over to the other woman.

CHAPTER 6

He'd been rude to Barbara Wilton, and he regretted it. Just because his anger about the threat to Aunt Ruth's home still simmered, he shouldn't be taking it out on her. Part of him wanted to go back and apologize, but that probably wouldn't be a great idea either.

He'd deal with it later. He had work to do

The address where the checks had been sent proved to be a small, run-down house at the end of a quiet street on the outskirts of town. The place sat by itself, maybe a quarter mile from its nearest neighbor. A mailbox bearing the house number but no name stood next to the driveway. When he stopped near it, he couldn't see any other homes through the thick stands of trees and shrubbery surrounding the place. Birds called in the trees and a squirrel chattered nearby, competing with the occasional distant rumble of traffic. Patchy grass in front of the place had grown long and full of weeds. A beat-up old pickup truck rusted forlornly toward the back, at the end of a long, unpaved drive. That rutted, weed-splotched length offered the only approach to the front door.

Chris got out and walked up to the house, cautious of where he put his feet on the rickety porch. Two of the posts on the railing had fallen out and a couple of the floorboards were visibly loose. He knocked on a front door that badly needed a new coat of paint. No one responded, even after a second knock. He yelled, "Hello?" and tried to peer through an uncurtained window, shielding his eyes from the sun as he did so. He could only make out a shadowy bit of a living room with a shabby couch and end table. Nothing moved inside though he waited for several minutes.

He walked back toward the car, stopping at the mailbox. The hinge squeaked, but the door opened onto an empty interior.

The next house on the street was larger, freshly painted, with a paved driveway, well-tended lawn, and a swing-set on the side. Flower beds along the front provided a colorful counterpoint to the white painted porch. A tricycle sat to one side. His knock on the door was answered quickly by a small child who yelled, "Mama!"

Moments later, a young woman holding a baby came to the door. She stood at the screen door and eyed him. "Yes?"

"Ma'am?" He introduced himself and said he needed to ask about the house down the street.

The woman nodded. "Come in if you want, but mind that the dog doesn't get out. Or any of the kids neither."

"This will only take a minute. Do you know who lives in the house down the street? Or if anyone is currently living there?" He pointed in the direction of the ramshackle building.

"Mr. Russell's place? Nobody's living there right now. Sam Russell's in a nursing home near Savannah. His mind's going and he broke his hip in a fall last year. His nieces or nephews come by occasionally to check up on the place and pick up any mail, but that's about it. Every now and again one will come and cut the grass, but it's been a while since they done that."

"You wouldn't happen to know the names of the nieces or nephews, would you?"

"No, I'm sorry. I talked with one of them one time, that's how I know about Mr. Russell, but I can't recall that I ever heard a name."

He stuck his card in the screen door. "Thank you. If you happen to remember a name, give me a call. Or if you see one of them, would you try to get a name for me?"

"Sure, deputy."

He sat in his car and typed a few notes into the computer mounted between the seats before he drove to the next place.

The garden and landscaping business was a large operation on the other side of town and some ways out. As he made his way to the customer service desk inside, a few people nodded in his direction and a couple gave him some dubious side-eye looks.

He asked for the manager at the service desk and the woman there paged Mr. Larkin. The name sounded familiar and he realized why when a man close to his own age approached. "Hey, Chris Harper," he said, holding out his hand. "Jim Larkin. I was a couple of years behind you in school. My older brother was in your class."

"Hal." Chris finally remembered why he recognized the name. "I remember him. You, too. You were on the baseball and football teams."

"Right. Never as good as you or Hal, though."

"I remember you were a pretty good center fielder."

"I did okay."

"And now you're the manager here," Chris asked.

"Yup. Got promoted last year."

Jim Larkin was developing a paunch and starting to lose some hair, but he remained as cheerful and friendly as Chris recalled him being.

"Congratulations."

Larkin eyed the badge on his chest. "I hear you're the deputy chief and acting sheriff right now."

"Until Will recovers from back surgery."

"You're here on official business?" Larkin asked. "I hope we don't have a problem."

"Yes, I'm here on business, but I don't think it's your problem. It's about a fraudulent check that was used here."

"Come on back to my office."

The man led the way through racks of garden tools, shelves of pots, and piles of bagged fertilizer to a tiny office, not much bigger than a closet. It had room for a desk, two chairs and a file cabinet with little maneuvering room. Larkin squeezed behind the desk then gestured to the other chair. "Have a seat and tell me what I can do to help."

Chris pulled out the copy of the check and

handed it to Larkin. "This was apparently written here and deposited by your company last month. We have reason to believe it was not signed by the people who own the account."

"Ralph and Della Percy. I know them, but I don't think I've ever seen them in here." Larkin stared at the paper a moment longer. "The cashiers are supposed to initial any checks they accept but I don't see that marked on here." He turned to the computer. "We don't get many checks anymore. Most people use credit cards. Let me pull up the sales report for that day."

"It would help if you could tell me who accepted the check and I could talk to them," Chris said.

Larkin scanned the screen. "I don't know if I can. I can find out what register it was in and who was working that day. We can narrow it down to maybe three or four possible people. But it's been more than a month. Odds are the person who took the check wouldn't even remember who gave it to them."

He got the names of the people working and found the proper register. "Okay, I'm looking at the sales receipt that check matches and it's odd. There are a couple of flats of plants and the rest is listed as 'miscellaneous.' A few things aren't in our database, but not many and at least two of them are included on the receipt. Plus there was a sixty dollar cash back. Now I really want to know who was responsible too. Something's fishy here."

Chris straightened and leaned forward.

Larkin pulled up another couple of reports and printed one out. He grabbed the sheet from the printer on a table next to his desk. "Here's a list of the employees who worked that day. Crossing out my name because I know I didn't take it and Jim Jenkins. He never works registers. That leaves four possibilities. I'm going to say it's not likely to be Gil. He's worked here for more than twenty years. Plus, I'm pretty sure he knows the Percys and he'd question it if someone else tried to pass off a check from them. Kate's here right now and Jason will be in later today. This one... Um, that's interesting. Dave quit about a week ago."

"Did he give a reason?"

"Got a better job offer from one of the big box places."

"Had he worked here long?"

"Maybe four months? We usually try to staff up in early spring and I'm pretty sure that's when I hired him."

"Got a full name and address there?"

The printer rattled out another sheet of paper, which Larkin passed to Chris. "You want to talk to Kate while you're here?"

Chris did. He talked to Gil, too. Both looked startled by the check. They both knew the Percys and each claimed they would have flagged any checks with their name passed by someone else. Their explanations didn't totally let either off the hook of possibly being part of a conspiracy, but neither seemed a likely candidate. If anyone at the store had been party to an effort to deliberately defraud the bank, and it now appeared probable that someone was, the former employee looked like the more viable option.

He next stopped in at the office to be sure no

drastic problems had developed in his absence. After going through his email and checking with dispatch, he returned a few phone calls, gobbled down the sandwich he'd made for lunch, and headed out again.

The address for Dave Vaughn was the middle unit of a set of three rickety looking apartments in a rundown part of town. No one answered when he knocked on the door, but an older man responded to his tap at the place on the left. The man opened up a crack barely wide enough for him to stare out warily. His eyes widened when he took in Chris's uniform and badge. "What you want?" he asked in a voice that quavered.

"I'm looking for the man next door," Chris said. "Dave Vaughn. I need to talk to him."

"Ain't seen him for a week or more," the old man said, holding the door open a few inches. "Thinking he skipped out on the rent."

"I heard he was working at one of the big box stores out on the highway?" Chris asked.

"Yeah. Wal-Mart, I think."

Chris thanked him, asked the old man to contact him if he did see Vaughn, and handed him a card. The door slammed shut the minute he turned away.

He got to his car in time to hear dispatch calling for any available units to handle a traffic accident. He responded along with a couple of others and the messy three-car pile-up engaged him for the rest of the afternoon.

As he drove home, his stomach tightened. He'd brought up the problems with Aunt Ruth to his mother the previous evening, but she'd been tired after a long day and didn't want to talk about it. He'd let it ride, knowing she needed time to absorb the issue. But time wasn't on their side and tonight he needed to press her on it. Decisions had to be made quickly if they were going to save Aunt Ruth's home.

His mom pulled a pan of meatloaf out of the oven as he walked into the kitchen. "If that tastes as good as it smells I can die happy tonight," he said, kissing her cheek.

"Don't be silly. Of course, it tastes as good as it smells."

He went to put away his weapons and change out of his uniform. By the time he returned, food sat on the table, ready for them. He let his mother guide the conversation for a while, talking about her day and what the neighbors were up to, until they'd mostly finished.

"We need to talk about Aunt Ruth and her house, Mom," he said. "We only have a few days to try to prevent it being foreclosed. But we need to talk about what to do about Aunt Ruth herself. Her memory's going. I'm not sure it's safe for her to stay there by herself much longer."

His mom chewed for a few moments, then drew in a long breath and set her fork down. "I know. But I have no idea what to do about any of it."

CHAPTER 7

Barbara woke on Saturday morning to a confused mix of feelings. She looked forward to a possibility of playing baseball again but dreaded it at the same time. If it had been a women's league or even a mixed league, she might not have been so nervous about it, even though she knew her skills were rusty. But playing with a group of men...

Carl, who'd invited her, had insisted she'd do fine. The team wasn't all that good anyway, so she couldn't really hurt it. Maybe he was right. She'd never know if she didn't try. What did she have to lose? Pride, dignity, self-esteem? None of those were tied up with her ability to play baseball. Not much anyway.

Fortunately Carl had prepared the way. When she got out of her car at the practice field he came over and said, "I told the guys you were coming and that you were pretty good. I see you got your own cleats. I'll get you a team shirt." He escorted her to where the men had congregated. She recognized a few of them from the bank. One was also on the July Fourth

Festival Committee. She shook hands as Carl introduced the others and told her what position they played. Most seemed open and friendly. Only Jerrold, the catcher, frowned as he shook hands and jerked his palm back within seconds.

She wanted to ask what his problem was, but Carl distracted her by asking. "Second base or left field?"

"My arm's too out of practice to play the outfield," she said.

"Second base it is," he said. He turned as another vehicle pulled into the parking lot. "Hey, here's an outfielder."

Barbara groaned as she recognized the truck. He'd mentioned that he'd played some. His work schedule probably didn't let him do it as regularly as he might've liked.

Chris stepped out of the truck, wearing jeans and a team tee shirt. He smiled at the other men, but his eyes widened when he saw her standing there. "We have a new recruit?"

Carl stepped up to answer. "Jack's down with a bad shoulder and Tom's visiting in-laws. We're never sure if you or Dave or Mickey can make it so we needed extra help. Besides I've seen her pitch and hit. She's good." His tone had a slight note of challenge, suggesting he was prepared for an argument about it.

Chris just smiled. "We need all the help all we can get."

Altogether they had ten people for practice. Barbara worried about her rusty skills. Mercifully her first fielding play was a ball squibbed so softly between first and second bases she had plenty of time to get her glove in position to scoop it up, transfer to her other hand, and toss it to the first basemen. Muscle memory took over and her body knew what to do. The next grounder was a little harder, but she was able to retrieve it. When a sharper hit went to the shortstop, she moved to cover second base, though the throw went to first. Then Jerrold clobbered a ball over her head into shallow right field. Barbara moved to cover second base and waved, noting that Jerrold was already rounding first. She took the throw from the right fielder and put a foot on the base two steps before Jerrold got there. He glared at her but turned and headed back to the dugout.

They had to stop practice for a few minutes when a stray dog wandered onto the field. None of the men recognized the shaggy beast and a couple tried to chase it off. The canine intruder retreated but started nosing around some of the bags the players had left at the side of the field. Probably a mix of several large breeds, the dog had matted, light brown fur over a body too thin for its size. The guys chased it away and the animal settled down in the shade of a tree off to the right of the field, apparently content to watch for a time.

Barbara took her turn at bat a few minutes later. Two pitches into it, one a ball and one a strike, she realized the pitcher was throwing much harder than he had earlier. Did having a woman at bat challenge him in a way that a man wouldn't? Or was the catcher, clearly hostile, directing the increase? No matter. The next two pitches were both balls, far enough outside the strike zone she didn't even offer at them.

Watching the pitcher's release gave her a hint of where the next ball would go. She shifted onto her back leg and raised the bat. She expected a curve ball and got one. At the point where it slid down into her happy zone, Barbara stepped into it, swung, and connected right at the sweet spot on the bat. The ball sailed over the infield, between center and left fielders and hit just below the top of the chain link fence that formed the outfield wall. She took off and slid into third well ahead of the throw from Chris, playing left field.

Carl was on third and he gave a shout as she stood up and brushed off dirt. "Nice piece of hitting! I knew you had it."

Several of the other players called congratulations as well.

Since they had so few players for practice, she didn't stay on base, but retrieved her glove and took over at third, so Carl could have a turn at bat.

The dog wandered back onto the field. A couple of the men tried to chase him away again, but he retreated under a bench and refused to budge. He growled when one tried to drag him out by the tail. "Hey, Harper," the man called. "Can you call Animal Control or just shoot the mutt? Get him away from here?"

Chris ran up and glared at the man. "I don't shoot animals unless they're going to be dinner or threatening someone. How do we know he doesn't belong to someone who's looking for him?"

"Don't see no collar on him."

The dog lifted a leg and scratched behind his ear. "Looks like he's got fleas and heaven only knows what else," the man added. The dog's short fluff didn't conceal that he was leaner than he should be.

Chris stared at the creature. "He doesn't look well cared for," he admitted. "It's Saturday and Animal Control is short-staffed right now. It'll be a good while before they can even get someone here."

Barbara didn't consider herself a dog person. Living in a city, she'd never thought about having a pet, since it would have to be cooped up all day in her small apartment, alone, while she went out to work. That didn't seem fair to any creature.

She stared at the dog, and he turned his head to meet her eyes. His tail started wagging slowly. Barbara went to her duffel bag and pulled out a bag of cheese crackers she'd packed as a snack. She took one and held it out.

The dog eyed her and started forward, then stopped, wary of a trap. Barbara waited. Moments later he crawled a few inches from under the bench, took the cracker, and crunched it up. He licked the ground to get every last crumb and looked up at her hopefully.

Carl took off his ball cap and wiped sweat from his face. "Reckon we're done here anyway. Getting too hot to practice. Game tomorrow night, everyone. I'll email details. Just two more after that. None next week on account of the Fourth of July holiday, but then Tuesday after that and the following Saturday." He looked at Barbara and said, "Give me your email address so I can include you."

She found a card in her duffel bag, wrote her private email address on the back, and handed it to him. Another cracker went to the dog, who crawled farther out from his shelter under the bench to take it from her. He didn't lunge or snap at the food she offered but accepted it gently.

The other players began to drift away, gathering their things, and getting in cars and trucks to drive off. Barbara gave the rest of the cheese crackers to the dog. A minute or two later both crackers and players were gone. Only she and Chris Harper remained at the field.

"I can't leave him like this," she said to Chris. "He's obviously hungry." She stared at the dog. "I don't know what to do. Could he belong to someone around here?"

They scanned the area. A few houses stood up the road, but the only other buildings nearby were a school building and a used car dealership beyond it.

"I doubt it," Chris said. "More likely he was abandoned. No collar and I don't think he's eaten for a while. Bet he needs water, too." He got a bottle he'd brought, still half full, poured some into his cupped hand, and held it out. The dog slurped it up, licking every last drop from Chris's palm and repeating that until the water was gone.

"What do we do with him?" she asked.

"Take him to the animal shelter, I guess," Chris said. "They can at least tell if he's micro-chipped. I kind of doubt it, though."

"If he's not?" Barbara stared at the dog, who looked back at her with eyes that begged for attention. Or maybe just more food.

"They'll hold him for a while. Try to find someone to adopt him."

"What are the odds of that?"

He shrugged and looked uncomfortable. "Probably not good."

"And if no one adopts him?"

While Chris stared off in the distance, clearly reluctant to answer, she felt a damp tongue lick her hand. The dog backed away again, tail down as if expecting a reprimand or worse after daring to touch her. "It's *not* a no-kill shelter, is it?" Her stomach clenched at the thought of this friendly animal being left to that fate.

He shook his head. "No." He sighed. "I can't take him home. My mother wouldn't have him in her house." He went to his truck and found some rope from a box in the bed. "I'll take him to the shelter. I can fashion a harness for him so we can put him in the back of the truck. Follow me or not if you want."

Barbara reached down to pat the dog's head. His tail wagged like a metronome when she scratched behind his ears. Chris wound the rope under his body behind his front legs then around in front in a complicated arrangement to form a makeshift harness. The dog followed him willingly to the truck and jumped in, tail still wagging while the ends of the rope were tied to hooks on the sides of the truck bed.

"I'll follow you," she said, gathering her duffel and getting into her own car.

CHAPTER 8

Chris recognized Nancy, the intake lady, as an old friend of his mother's. Nancy ran a gloved hand over the dog's fur and scanned him with a small machine that beeped when she turned it on. "No micro-chip, I'm afraid. He's under-nourished, has fleas and mange and probably some other things. Almost certainly a stray or abandoned a while back. But he has good manners so he may have been a pet at some time."

"People abandon their pets?" Barbara sounded shocked.

"All the time," Nancy answered. "It's sad, isn't it?"

"It is." Barbara stared at the dog with compassion and something more.

Nancy saw it, too. "Would you want to consider fostering him, while we search for a forever home for him? We work with a couple of rescue services that would help sponsor it."

"What does it involve?"

"The good thing is that if you agree to foster, the service will help cover his vet bills and provide some equipment. You'll have to leave him here for a few days while we get him cleaned up and ready, but then you take him home and love him until we find someone to adopt." Nancy smiled wryly. "Of course, that's the down-side. You have to give him up when he is adopted."

"But what if he isn't?" Barbara asked.

"Then you can either decide to adopt him yourself or he comes back to the shelter."

"I can decide to adopt him?"

"Any time." She grinned. "We call that a 'failed fostering,' but in truth we're all delighted when it happens."

Barbara looked torn. "I don't even know if my lease allows pets."

Chris wished he could do something more helpful. The dog had touched her heart, and for some reason that drew her into his. "You have a good-sized yard," he said. "I'll bet it does."

"I don't know anything about dogs. What to feed them, exercise, training, any of that."

"We'll help you out with that," Nancy said.

"I will, too." Chris almost kicked himself even as he was saying the words. Where had that come from? He had enough on his plate already, but the mutt had dug his way into his heart, too, maybe because Barbara Wilton had— Oh, no, he wasn't going there.

He looked at his watch. "I've got to get going. Have a meeting at three and I need to clean up before it. As a matter of fact..." He looked at Barbara. "Aren't you on the Fourth Festival Planning Committee?"

Dismay flashed across her face. "Omigosh. I am. And I was about to totally forget it. I need to shower first, too."

Nancy was ready. "Why don't you think about it and check your lease, and I'll call you Monday morning. I'll start the process on the assumption you're going to foster him, but you're not committed to it."

"Okay," Barbara agreed.

"Oh," Nancy said. "We need a name for him. Do you have any ideas?"

Barbara hesitated for a moment. "We found him on a ball field. How about we name him after my favorite player? Mookie."

"Mookie Betts?" Chris asked.

She nodded.

"Mookie, it is," Nancy said, writing it down. Barbara watched as Nancy guided Mookie off the table and into the back. As they passed through the door, the dog glanced back, giving him, then Barbara a soulful look.

Barbara sighed when they disappeared, then shook herself and said, "I guess we better get going."

As he held the shelter door for her to exit, she said, "I didn't realize you were on the committee. I haven't seen you at the meetings before."

"I'm not really. But the sheriff always meets with them to make sure everything is coordinated for road closures for the parade and traffic control. Since the sheriff is currently incapacitated, it's my job." He escorted her to her car and said, "I'll see you there."

When he got home twenty minutes later, his mother was out. He put together a quick sandwich, then showered and put on his uniform. He checked in at the office, to find everything quiet. After answering a few emails, he headed across the street to the city hall building and the large conference room at the back.

Most of the committee and subcommittee members had already gathered. This was the last meeting before the Fourth Festivities on Wednesday, and he felt tension in the air, with everyone anxious to be sure all their bases were covered.

He couldn't help looking around for Barbara. She sat near the middle of one long side of the enormous table. Noticing him, she gave him a nod and a small smile, but at that moment, Mary Jo Ryder, the chairwoman, called the meeting to order. He took a seat away from the table, near the side of the room.

They went through several issues, covering finances for the event and publicity, before Mary Jo called on him to review the safety and traffic control plans. He went over diagrams showing the parade route and which streets would be closed off, where parking was available, and a final one that outlined the festival grounds, where the stage for the musical performances would be and locations of games and food booths. He promised that all deputies would be on hand along with a few state troopers who would join them to help keep order.

As he finished his talk, he let himself look at Barbara again, meeting her gaze. She broke the contact after a moment, but not before he read the attraction in her eyes that mirrored what he felt. He suspected she wasn't any happier about it than he was.

He scanned the people at the table and noted that a couple of others looked from him to Barbara and back. No doubt he'd just fueled a grand spate of rumor and speculation on the town grapevine.

He sat down to listen to the rest of the meeting. Most of it bored him, but he did pay more attention when Barbara gave her report on the final registration numbers for parade modules and festival booths. He was surprised they hadn't made her the treasurer for the whole thing, but he realized why when they got to the report on the funds. Cindy Martinson already had that job, not surprising, since she also worked at the bank, and had likely been in the festival position for years.

Another uncomfortable realization hit him as he watched Cindy give her report. The woman kept looking his way, forcing him to remember several times in the last few months when she'd struck up conversations on seeing him nearby. It had started when he'd taken a couple of the younger deputies for pizza. One of them was a relative of hers, and he'd introduced them that evening after he saw her enter alone.

Although they'd gone to school together, she'd been three years behind him, so he barely remembered her. But since then, she'd conveniently shown up a couple of times when he'd stopped for coffee at Latte Da and had invited herself to join him.

He'd thought it just small-town friendliness on her part. His failure to recognize her crush probably resulted from his insulating himself from any emotional entanglements since the divorce. He hoped he could let her down gently. But she worked at the bank with Barbara, and that could be an issue if Cindy saw his friendship with the other woman in the wrong light.

He'd lost the thread of the meeting, but when he realized they were wrapping up, he decided to duck out early.

The day had remained quiet, so he ventured home for dinner with his mom. She made her famous tomato vegetable soup and some fresh bread to go with it. A simple meal but delicious. Once they'd sat down and blessed the food, he asked, "Have you thought any more about Aunt Ruth and the house?"

"I haven't thought of much else for the last couple of days. But I don't know what to do. I hate to even think of selling that house, but what other options are there?"

"I don't know," Chris admitted. "And I hate to have to move her, but I'm not sure it's safe to leave her there alone, on top of the financial problems. I checked and she's missed two payments on the power bill in the last year. Right now she's still a month behind."

His mother sighed loudly. "Can we even convince her to sell the house before the bank forecloses?"

"I don't think we have that kind of time. At this point I think our only choices are to let it go to foreclosure or come up with the money to get the mortgage up to date. If we get it up to date, then we can make the decision to sell or not." He ate a few spoonsful of soup in silence, then asked, "Mom, do you know if Aunt Ruth has any savings, or any money put away?"

"I don't know, but I don't think so. She once told me all she had was Sherm's pension and his social security."

Chris set down his spoon and tapped his fingers on the table as he thought. "The divorce pretty much wiped me out. I have a couple of thousand in my 401K, but taxes will eat that up if take it out."

"I could probably scrape the money together, but it would take all my savings."

"The savings for that trip you're going to take to Paris some day?" Chris asked. "No way. You're not touching that."

"But I can't let Ruth lose the house. It's been in her husband's family for three generations."

"She doesn't have any children to leave it to," Chris said. "It would probably get sold anyway."

His mother gave him an odd look. "She never told you?"

"Told me what?"

"It's supposed to go to you. You're her only blood relative left in the next generation."

He'd never even considered that possibility. "Didn't Sherm have some cousins or something? Shouldn't it go to them?"

"None of them ever gave Ruth the time of day. It irritated Sherm. He wanted her to leave it to you when it was clear they wouldn't have any children of their own."

Chris sighed. "As inheritances go, this one is a bit of an albatross. It might be better to let it go into foreclosure."

His mother gasped. "You can't. Chris, you can't. It would kill Ruth."

"I know, Mom," he said. "I just don't know how to avoid it."

"You need to ask your pretty banker friend for advice. She deals with these things. She probably has some suggestions for you."

Chris tapped the table with his fingertips again. He really didn't want to go to Barbara Wilton, begging for help. But what choice did he have? He stopped tapping and considered another option. He'd promised to help her with the dog. No doubt, she'd be grateful for the assistance. In return, she could help him with the foreclosure. A deal. He'd be making a deal with her.

CHAPTER 9

Barbara rounded up her papers as the Planning Committee meeting came to an end. She had to get her head sorted out. That look she'd shared with Chris rattled her on a bone-deep level. She thought she'd been successful in resisting the man's appeal, but the emotions she read in his expression, the heartache coupled with something that looked like longing, curled their way into her heart. Everything about Chris Harper attracted her—his looks, the concern for his family that revealed a kind heart, the deep integrity she'd sensed made up his backbone, even the hints of suffering that showed how much he could care.

But. She didn't dare let another man into her life. She'd been burned twice. How many times did life have to teach her the dangers of letting yourself care for someone?

But. But... He wasn't just any man. Chris Harper was a special kind of man. Not the sort you ran across every day or every month, or even every year.

"Hey, Barb?" Cindy's voice drew her out of the painful introspection.

She tried to summon a smile for the other woman. "Hi Cindy. What is it?"

"I noticed that a couple of the registrations you gave me didn't have payments with them. I was trying to sort out the finances for the committee and wondered if you'd made any special arrangements with some people? It looks like it was two of the food booths."

Barbara paused for a moment. "I gave you the payments for all of the registrations. I didn't make any special arrangements. They were all paid for. I noted on the forms how they were paid and attached cash or checks to them. And I handed it all onto you."

"Are you sure? There are two payments I don't seem to have."

"You've double-checked?" Barbara asked. "I'm sure I gave it all to you."

"I've looked around, but I can't find those two payments."

She sighed, puzzled, suspicious, and impatient, but she controlled the emotions. "Which ones are they? I'll check my folders. See if they got detached from the copy of the registration."

"Good idea." Cindy showed her the two forms missing payments and Barbara noted down names, dates, and numbers. "Check around wherever you've been keeping them, too," she asked.

Barbara wasn't sure what else to say. She knew she'd attached those payments along with the others. Since this was her first time working on a project like this, she'd been extra careful. But she'd still check that they hadn't accidently gotten left somewhere in the folder or drawer.

Alarm bells rang in the back of her mind as she recalled Sheila's warning. She had the copies she'd made and she'd handed off the forms in front of people in the bank, but in fact, neither of those could totally prove she'd turned the money over.

The missing payments occupied her thoughts until she got home. She went straight to her desk and pulled out the folders where she'd kept the registrations. Nothing sat beneath them in the drawer. Flipping through each packet didn't reveal any missing or misplaced payments. Barbara turned on her computer and brought up the spreadsheet where she'd recorded the registrations and payments. Most of the registrations had been done online, but she'd printed copies of each. The payments had also largely been by credit card and processed through an online payment system she'd set up. Those payments were forwarded directly to the Festival Committee's bank account, and she would note the payment details on the registration form. Of the two Cindy had said were missing, one was done by check, the other in cash. She remembered the cash payment with its fat wad of bills. She'd been careful with it, fastening the money to the form with a binder clamp. Tracey had witnessed her counting the cash and locking it up with the forms the day she'd handed it over.

No way she'd lost that money herself. Something must've happened to it after she'd passed it on. But how could she prove it?

Unless the transfer had been caught on camera—which was a possibility—and clear enough to show the cash attached—not likely, unfortunately—she had no actual proof she'd given it to Cindy. She couldn't access the bank video to check. Only the police, with a warrant, could do that. She'd tried to be sure the hand-off was public, but the video likely wouldn't show enough detail to prove the payments were there.

Barbara didn't like the ugly suspicion growing in her mind as she considered what might've happened to the money. The missing amount wasn't huge, but it wasn't her money—or Cindy's, and it would represent a significant loss to the Committee's charities.

What could she do? She mulled over various ways to handle the situation, but none were great. If Cindy insisted the money hadn't been attached, Barbara might not have any good defense. It could come down to her word against Cindy's, and she was an outsider, a recent transplant, while Cindy had grown up in this town. No question whose side most people would take.

She stuck a frozen chicken dinner in the microwave while musing on the problem. No answers – easy or otherwise – presented themselves to her. She didn't even know who she could talk with about it.

While eating, she tried to lose herself in another of the books Edie had convinced her to buy. The story absorbed her enough to distract her during dinner, but when she stood up afterward, the worries crashed back in. Not just the missing money issue, but also the question of what to do about Mookie. Even if her lease permitted it, should she agree to foster the dog? She'd get attached. Right now, she might – maybe – be able to let him go.

Who was she kidding? Mookie had already worked his way under her skin. Leaving him with the shelter meant at least decent odds he wouldn't survive long. She couldn't let him be euthanized. But could she take care of a dog? The lease would make the choice, she decided. If she couldn't have a pet, that made the decision for her.

Once she'd cleaned up from dinner, she dug a copy of the lease agreement out of her files and read through. Nowhere did it say anything about animals. It didn't make the harder decision of what to do if he weren't adopted, but she'd deal with that later. Monday morning, she'd let the shelter know she'd agree to fostering. And Chris Harper had offered to help her with the dog, a good thing, since she knew almost nothing about caring for canines.

Getting back into her book that evening took work, but the story Edie had recommended sucked her in and involved her until bedtime.

Her Little League team had a game the next afternoon, on a Sunday where temperatures peaked in the high eighties. She brought a case of bottled water in a cooler, as did the other coaches. One of the challenges of coaching in summer in the south was being sure the kids drank enough to stay hydrated.

As sometimes happened, only one official showed up for the game, so the coaches took it in turns to stand in for a second one.

Her turn, in the fifth and sixth innings,

stayed routine until the bottom of the sixth when one of her own players got a solid hit. Barbara moved from behind first to second base as the runner approached. The other team's second baseman also ran to cover, with the ball and runner both closing quickly on the base. The runner dove head-first and slid into second. The play was close, but Barbara was convinced the runner's hand had caught the bag before the tag was applied and she ruled him safe.

She expected the resulting boos and jeers from parents of the other team's players. The approach of the opposing coaches didn't shock her. Both were red-faced and angry, arguing loudly that the runner was out. Barbara remained calm in the heat of their anger, explaining that in her judgement, the runner had touched the base prior to the tag. Neither was buying it, but she also knew they could do nothing about it. Her word was final.

Unless they could intimidate her into changing her call, and they tried to do just that. She didn't blame them for it, as long as they used words. What she couldn't and wouldn't tolerate was the third-base coach grabbing her arm and trying to shake her to get her to change her mind. To his credit, the head coach immediately pulled the other man back and away from her.

The threat of physical violence had rattled her, but there were rules and consequences. No one was allowed to lay hands on an official— male or female, not at any level of baseball, from the major leagues on down. "You're out," she told the coach, making the gesture that signaled he was ejected from the game.

The home plate official ran up to support her, also signaling that the coach who'd grabbed her was tossed from the game.

"She was right about the call," he said. "I had a good angle on it, too, though from further away. He was safe."

The coach she'd tossed walked away muttering "girls don't belong in baseball."

Barbara ignored him. The parents of the other team still yelled insults and booed, but Barbara refused to acknowledge them either. The thought that some of them might be bank customers crossed her mind. She hoped they'd understand that she really was trying to be fair. Umpires had a hard job.

Two more hits from their team in the inning put them up by two runs but the only other close play was at home plate and not her call.

She finished the rest of her officiating stint without further incident. "Sorry about that nitwit," Carl told her when she returned to her team's bench. "Tig Robbins is a bully. Has been for as long as I've known him. Glad you didn't let him intimidate you."

"It was close. I was worried a riot might break out."

"Nah. Not happening. We've got law enforcement present."

"What?" She looked around. Her heart leapt at the possibility of Chris Harper's presence, but the uniformed deputy standing near his car by the entrance to the field was much younger and a stranger. "Someone call them?"

"I did. They usually have someone nearby when we're playing. Sadly this isn't the first incident. We once had parents actually throwing bottles and cans onto the field. That was a couple years ago. We had to call the game and it went down as a forfeit for the home team."

The rest of the time passed without incident. Her team won and she was especially proud of the play of a couple of kids she'd coached. Seeing the youngsters improve was one of the main joys of her volunteering to help the team. She went home and debated about showering. She'd be getting hot and sweaty again that evening, playing with the men's team. But the salty coating on her skin made her uncomfortable. Eating dinner that way wouldn't be fun, and she didn't want to show up to the next game with greasy hair, so she stepped under the hot water to rinse off.

Walking back through the living room to the kitchen, she pictured where the dog's crate and bed would go. The house had the advantage of a fenced back yard and a few trees, but she didn't want to leave him outside all the time to bake in the summer Georgia sun. She'd need to get a crate, a leash, dog dishes, food, probably other things, too. She made a note to ask what the shelter or rescue service would supply and what she'd have to buy on her own.

Another frozen dinner went in the microwave, but she did fix herself a salad to go with it, if pouring shredded, mixed lettuce out of a bag from the grocery store counted as doing it herself. She poured a balsamic vinegar dressing over it and pulled the tray with meat lasagna out of the oven. It had a side of green beans she planned to ignore and a brownie that took an effort of will to save until last.

Afterward, she cleaned up the kitchen, changed her current t-shirt for the team one, grabbed the bag with her cleats, cap, mitt, water bottles, and a few other necessities, and drove to the ball field.

As the "new guy" she expected that she wouldn't be in the starting lineup unless they were actually short a player, and she was right. She and another young man sat on the bench in the dugout as the game started. Chris had arrived shortly after she did. She wanted to talk to him, but he was immediately pulled into a discussion with another player that lasted until the game started.

The young man who shared the bench with her gave her an awkward look. "Hi, Ms. Wilton. We met at practice the other night, but I doubt you remember me. Tyler Vickers."

"I remember you. You're a relief pitcher, right?"

"And backup for the outfield," he said, "but I prefer pitching."

"I understand. I've done some relief pitching, too." She smiled at him. "I have a favor to ask."

"Sure." He seemed to relax. "What is it?"

"Call me Barbara. We're on the same team. 'Ms. Wilton' makes me feel way too old to being playing baseball."

"Oh, but you're not too old," he said, hastily. "Not old at all. Barbara. It's just that you are older than me." He grinned again and a flush of pink washed over his cheeks.

Barbara eyed him. "Bet I'm five years older than you. Not all that big a gap."

"I'm twenty-three," he said.

"Okay. I'm wrong. It's six years. Still not a big gap."

The first half of the first inning ended, and all the rest of the team's players crowded into the dugout except the first man up to bat and the one warming up on deck. Several of them greeted Barbara and made various comments. A couple asked if she was ready for the Fourth Festival. There seemed to be a lot of excitement about it.

When the team was on the field, she mostly sat with Tyler, talking about the game, the players, and the strategy. She didn't get any time with Chris until the second half of the fifth inning, when he came over and sat with her. "Made any decisions about the mutt?" he asked.

"My lease doesn't say anything about pets, so I'm going to try fostering him. I'll let them know about it tomorrow."

"You're sure you're okay with it? If you have to give him up to an adoptive family?"

"It'll be hard," she admitted. "But I'll also be happy to know he'll have a good home."

"That's a good attitude. I hope—"

They were interrupted when Carl came over and said, "Barbara, do you think you could handle third base? Jeff thinks he may have tweaked his knee. He's gonna give it a go next inning, but he's not sure how much he can do."

Barbara refused to let any doubts show. "I'll give it my best try."

Carl looked at Tyler. "I'm giving Jeff one more inning pitching, then I want you to go in. Start warming up."

"I'll catch for you," Barbara said. The field

didn't have a bullpen, so they went to an open area outside the fence. Tyler's pitches were erratic, at best, but Barbara corralled most of them. When one or two escaped, Tyler ran after and retrieved the ball.

She noticed a couple of things about his pitching motion, but hesitated before asking, "Do you mind if I make a suggestion?" He didn't seem offended by the idea, so she continued. "I notice you're falling off to the left after you release the ball. Can you try to not twist so much and extend your arm more toward home plate when you follow through?"

He looked surprised, then nodded. And he made an effort to do as she suggested. The first couple of pitches went wildly astray, though Barbara snagged both. But then he began to feel what she meant, and the next few throws were over the plate. Their time ran out as the inning ended and they both took the field.

Third base wasn't a position she'd played much, but she'd watched the other team long enough to know only two of their members could hit decently, and both had been up to bat in the previous inning. She only had to field two hits in the rest of the game, both weak ground balls. One took so long to get to her, the batter had rounded first and unwisely decided to try to stretch his single into a double. She threw the ball to second, the player covering caught it and tagged the runner out by several steps. The other play that came to her required a longer throw that landed a couple of feet in front of the first baseman. It didn't matter. The runner had already beaten the throw.

She got only one chance at bat, and she hit

a slow roller between first and second. The second basemen threw her out at first. In the end, they lost the game by two runs, but there were some hopeful notes. The team they lost to was the second best in their league and they'd been competitive. Carl came and asked, "What did you tell Tyler? That's the best I've ever seen him pitch."

She explained what she'd seen and how he was trying to correct the problem. Carl shook his head but said, "I'd never noticed, but now you mention it, it's true. Good spotting."

Chris had listened in, and he added a comment. "Thanks for that. I think you increased Tyler's confidence a couple of hundred percent."

The others began to depart after Carl's reminder that they'd practice again the following Saturday. Chris's truck was parked next to her car, so they walked there together. As she reached the door of her Honda, he stopped and said, "We need to talk. You said you had some questions about taking care of the dog, and I need your help figuring out how to stave off foreclosure on Aunt Ruth's house. Do you think you might be able to do dinner with me tomorrow night? I thought we might try for one of the nice restaurants in Savannah?"

Dinner with him at a nice restaurant? Her heart slammed a hard beat and picked up speed. Breath caught in her throat for a moment. "Sounds wonderful," Barbara finally said. The words came out calmer than she expected.

Sounded dangerous as well. Too much like a

date. But even if she didn't need his help with the dog, she still couldn't pass up the chance to get to know Chris Harper better.

He smiled that wonderful grin that showed his dimples to full effect and made his blue eyes sparkle. "Terrific. I'll pick you up at six."

CHAPTER 10

Chris went into the office on Monday morning, still pinching himself to be sure he wasn't dreaming. Barbara Wilton had agreed to have dinner with him that evening. It wasn't really a date, though. They had things to discuss and doing it over dinner just made sense. He called to make a reservation for two at a highly recommended restaurant in Savannah. He'd need to get ready quickly when he got home from work. Not a date, though. Was he kidding himself?

He had a few administrative tasks to handle before he resumed the search for Dave Vaughn, who might be connected with a fraudulent check scheme. So he was in his office, reviewing reports, when Barbara called to tell him she was set up as a temporary foster parent for Mookie.

"I won't be able to bring him home until tomorrow but they're providing most of the equipment they said I'd need. And a bag of food." She hesitated a moment before adding, "I'm kind of terrified. I don't know anything about dogs."

"You'll do fine. I'll fill you in more tonight, but, honestly, dogs aren't hard to care for. Food, water, exercise, and loving. That about covers what they need."

"Okay. Thanks for the reassurance. I'll see you tonight." She didn't actually sound all that reassured.

"Is something else bothering you?" he asked.

"I don't know. Maybe. We can talk about it tonight."

"Okay." He reminded her he'd pick her up at six and hung up.

After finishing the paperwork, he called the Walmart outside town to ask about Dave Vaughn. After a couple of transfers, he was connected to the manager and identified himself. The woman sighed when he asked if David Vaughn worked there."

"No, he doesn't. Not anymore."

"Something happened?"

"I'm not supposed to discuss personnel matters," she said.

"I'm a deputy sheriff, investigating a crime. I can get a warrant if I need to."

"No, don't bother." The woman sighed. "There was a fuss about a check he accepted. He failed to follow proper procedure with it, and it bounced. He didn't try to deny it and was defiant about the whole thing, so his employment was terminated."

"I see. Do you have any contact information for him?"

She gave him the same useless address and phone number he already had. He thanked her and ended the call. He checked various databases and search engines but none helped him locate the man. He gave up and declared Dave Vaughn a dead end. For the moment anyway.

It took three tries at various nursing homes around Savannah to locate one that had a patient named Sam Russell. Chris scheduled an appointment to talk with him later in the week, though the staff warned the man's memories were spotty at best.

At five, he headed home to shower and change out of his uniform into dark slacks and a dress shirt. He took a sport coat and tie with him but elected not to wear them. Few places were that formal in Georgia in July.

Still, he felt under-dressed and a little outclassed when Barbara opened the door for him. She wore a simple, sleeveless violet sheath dress that molded her lithe figure beautifully. Medium-heeled pumps put her nearly at eye-level with him, and her hair was pulled back off her face in a complicated twist. Dangly earrings and a long, silver chain necklace completed the look.

He stood still in awe. For a few moments he couldn't say anything at all, could barely breathe. "You look amazing," he said when he finally was able to form words again.

"Thank you. You look good yourself," she answered.

They kept the conversation light on the drive into Savannah. He asked if she'd rooted for the Red Sox all her life.

"I have," she answered. "It's like a family tradition. And I'm betting you're a Braves fan?"

"Of course. This is Georgia. You may find a

scattering of fans of the Florida teams, but we mostly support the Braves. It's sort of expected."

"Ever been to a game?" she asked.

"Braves? A few times." He told her about a couple of occasions when he and his father had driven to Atlanta to take in a game, and she traded stories of trips to Fenway Park.

When she asked about his work, he related some of the funnier stories and situations he'd encountered. They laughed for much of the trip to the restaurant.

Once there, they were escorted immediately to a table that looked out a window over the river. They each asked for a glass of wine along with their dinners. Once the server had taken their orders, he asked, "What is the shelter giving you for Mookie?"

"Actually I think it's a rescue service providing the stuff, but they said he'd have a crate, cushion, a harness, leash, and a bag of dog food. He'll be wearing a cone for a few days since they 'fixed' him, and they're providing some medicine I'm supposed to give him."

She looked up at him, her brown eyes wide and filled with doubt. "How do I give a dog medicine? How do I do anything with a dog? I've never had one."

"Don't panic. It's not hard to give a dog medicine. They'll probably be pills and you can put one in with his kibble when you feed him. If he doesn't gulp it down along with the rest of his food, you can try coating it with peanut butter to give him as a treat."

"Peanut butter is okay for dogs?"

"I'm pretty sure it is. Chocolate's the big no-

no as far as I remember."

"You've had dogs before?"

"We usually had one or two around when I was growing up," he said. "Until my dad died. He was the one who took care of them."

"You miss him?"

"My dad. A lot. But it's been almost ten years now. I wish he was still around, but it doesn't hurt anymore. Anyway, taking care of the dogs wasn't really a big deal. He'd give them food and water, let them run around for a while, make sure they had a sheltered place to sleep at night. Took them to the vet every now and again when they needed it."

"Okay. What do I feed him? And how much?"

"They're giving you some food. Just ask how much they recommend for him and how often. You can buy more at the grocery store. Before or after you pick him up, you'll want to buy a bag of treats to use for training him, food and water bowls, and a few toys. If you're going to let him stay inside, you'll need to walk him a couple of times a day or turn him out into the yard to do his business. Presuming he's already house-trained. I'll come over tomorrow evening, if that's okay with you and we can go over anything else that's needed."

The look of relief on her face rewarded him for giving up some free time.

"I'd be so grateful," she said. "I'm going to leave work early to pick him up."

The server arrived with their drinks and a basket of bread, so they took a moment to appreciate them. He lifted his glass. "A toast to helping each other?"

She smiled and the beauty of it stabbed right

into him. "To helping each other."

They each took a sip. He made sure his hand didn't betray the tremor running through him.

Then she asked, "Have you decided what you want to do about your aunt's house?"

"I've had several talks with my mom. She's wrestling with it. The decisions aren't easy. But we want to keep the house. And we'd like to keep Aunt Ruth in it for as long as possible. Mom's talked to her and thinks she can convince her we should move in with her. She's making it sound like Aunt Ruth would be doing us a favor by letting us stay with her. My mom doesn't have the same kind of attachment to the house she's in now as Aunt Ruth does hers. In fact, Mom has talked about selling the house for some time, although she gave up the idea when I moved back. I suspect if I were to move out on my own, she would go ahead and unload it. The problem is she probably can't get through the paperwork for a sale fast enough to get the money in time."

"Probably not," Barbara agreed. "And even things like short-term loans can take time, if they're from a legitimate lender."

"I can pull about three thousand out of an IRA," he said, "and Mom said she has about three thousand stashed away in an emergency fund. But that still leaves us a bit over three thousand short. Mom's talking about pawning some of her jewelry. I'm trying to talk her out of it."

The server arrived with their meals then and they took a couple of minutes to enjoy the food and take the edge of their appetites before continuing the conversation.

Barbara stared at him, and her lips twisted as though she didn't like what she was about to say. "I hope this isn't too personal or impertinent a question, but why are you struggling so hard to keep someone else's house? You could move your Aunt Ruth in with your mother, couldn't you? If you do rescue the house from foreclosure, what happens when your aunt passes away? If she leaves it to someone else or a charity or something, you won't recover any of the money you invested."

"It's a good question, not impertinent at all. I'm telling you this in confidence, so please keep it to yourself. I don't want anyone in town to know right now. According to my mom, Aunt Ruth plans to leave the house to me."

"I see. Does she have a will? And is it spelled out there? I know this sounds cold and crass, but you need to think about it. Before you invest your savings and your mother's, you should make sure of your facts, or you could be putting yourself in a difficult situation."

"Good point. I'll ask Mom to check on that."

"You'll want to be sure about it before turning over any money. Even then—she could change the will and you'd be stuck. But I guess you have to have some trust in your family. You should also check on what resources your aunt might have to contribute herself. If she hasn't been paying her bills, she may have money built up in an account somewhere."

"Another good idea," he said. "We have no idea what she's been doing with the money she gets from Uncle Sherm's pension and social security. She might have given it all away for all we know."

"You know, if she's showing signs of dementia, you and your mother might need to take a closer look at her finances. Maybe consider if you should get a power of attorney. And make sure she already has a will or makes one right away while she still can."

He nodded and she continued. "But here's what I can do to help. I can call the bank that holds the mortgage, explain the situation, and ask for a bit more time. Because I work for this branch bank myself, I think they'll listen and may be more sympathetic. Also—and I don't know if they'll agree to this or not—I'll try to talk them into accepting back payments in two or three installments, spaced over a few months."

"That would be incredibly helpful." He reached across the table to touch her hand. "Thank you." He kept the contact brief, though he wanted to leave his fingers on hers. Her hand was warm and soft, and he felt an odd buzz vibrate between them.

They ate in silence for a while. The server came to ask if they wanted anything else and he looked to Barbara. "Dessert?"

"No thanks. No room."

"Why don't we walk for a while. The River Walk is right there, and it's a beautiful evening."

"I'd love to," Barbara answered.

After he paid for dinner, they stood and left the restaurant. A hot day had turned into a pleasant twilight. The sun neared the horizon to the west, and with its passing, the daytime heat faded into more moderate, if still somewhat humid, warmth.

Heavy pedestrian traffic, interspersed with bikers, skateboarders, and a few people on roller blades, meant they made slow, cautious progress for the first twenty minutes. They paused a couple of times to watch street performers, a pair of clever jugglers, and a one-man band. The occasional shop drew their attention with intriguing gift ideas and souvenirs.

They walked in silence for a few minutes longer, until they reached a quieter, less trafficked stretch of the path. He helped her down a couple of steps and kept her hand in his when they resumed walking. She didn't object or try to pull away. In a corner of his mind, he recognized the deep, personal nature of that contact, and that in his offering and her accepting, they had each moved a step closer to a relationship neither of them was sure they wanted. He told himself it wasn't a big deal, just a man and woman holding hands. But it was.

"Earlier today you said something was bothering you, but you didn't say what. Is it something you can talk about?" he asked.

For a few long moments she remained quiet, long enough for him to begin to regret asking the question.

"This is awkward," she said, slowly. "I can't tell you about this without sounding like I'm accusing someone else of…something. And I don't want to do that, because I can't be sure of anything. Or at least I can't prove even what I am sure of."

"That's kind of confusing."

She huffed out a harsh laugh. "I know. I'll try to keep names out of this except for mine. On the July Fourth Festival Committee, I was in charge of the registrations and collecting the fees for the booths. Most of the fees were paid online by credit card, so no problem there, but a few were paid with checks and a couple even with cash. I kept careful records of what I collected and kept the payments with the registration forms. Those were handed on to – someone else – to be deposited in the Festival account. But that someone told me that some of the payments were missing from the material I gave her. I checked to be sure they hadn't gotten left in the drawer or the folders, even though I didn't think that could have happened. And it didn't. I'm sure of it. But this other person is implying that I failed to turn over the money to her, for whatever reason. And, while I have good records and witnesses who saw me hand the papers to her, I don't really have any way to prove I actually gave her all the money. It's going to come down to my word against hers, and this other person is a long-time resident of the town."

"I see." And he did. He briefly tightened his grip on her hand, a gesture he meant to be reassuring. "I'm pretty sure I know who this 'somebody else' is. And the situation may not be exactly what you think, though I can understand why you believe what you do." He struggled with what to tell her. He wanted to make her feel better without compromising any ongoing investigations. Sort of ongoing, anyway, although sputtering along for several years might be more accurate. "Mary Jo Ryder is still the head of the Festival Committee, isn't she?"

"Yes."

"Here's what I think you should do. Tell Mary Jo what's happening. Feel free to name names since she knows who's doing what anyway."

"Why would she believe me?"

"I've known her for years. She's a smart lady. And you'd be wise to tell her first, before 'someone else' has a chance to complain to her. I can't say for sure what she'll believe, but I do think she has good judgement."

She hesitated for a moment before saying, "That sounds like good advice."

"I try," he said.

They strolled in silence for a while as the sky darkened into night. He found it surprisingly comfortable to walk hand in hand with her, admiring the beauty of the night sky and the reflections in the river, sneaking occasional sideways glances at the woman beside him who eclipsed both sky and river. "Can I ask a favor?"

He could just make out her face in the light from a distant lamp pole as she answered, "Sure. You can ask."

"Don't judge the whole town on the actions of one individual. And don't assume we're so insular that we'll automatically side with a local no matter what the circumstances."

"I don't judge the town at all. I know every place has its good and bad, and people with all sorts of issues. And honestly, pretty much everyone has been welcoming, so I can't really complain." She turned toward him and squeezed his hand. "I'm sure I don't have to tell you about the people with issues."

A light breeze caressed them as they walked. "No. Although it's nothing like it was in

Charlotte, people still pick on each other, fight, occasionally take what doesn't belong to them, and even write bad checks."

"Do you miss working in Charlotte?" she asked.

He'd asked himself that question a couple of times and still wasn't sure of the answer. "Sometimes, I do. I miss the action, the camaraderie with other officers, the feeling that I was protecting people, and the never-a-slow-moment nature of the days. On the other hand, I don't miss the physical violence, the actual danger, the general nastiness of it sometimes. I'm not an adrenaline junkie, but I don't like being bored either."

"Would you go back if your family didn't need you?"

That was the core difficulty at the heart of any relationship they might have. He considered what to say. "The most honest answer I can give you at this point is: I don't know. There's a lot to be said for Willow Ridge. I feel like I can be an important part of the community and make a difference here, where in Charlotte I was a cog in the machine. And I still hope to have a family. Willow Ridge is a good place to raise kids."

He waited to see if she'd release his hand, but she didn't. She squeezed it again and they continued in silence for a while.

CHAPTER 11

Barbara woke up the next morning, still basking in the glow from the previous evening. The night had been almost perfect. A great dinner and a wonderful walk on a clear, moonlit night, holding hands with Chris Harper. They'd talked and laughed and shared some personal things about themselves and offered each other the benefit of their different experiences.

No matter that her pretty Stuart Weitzman pumps weren't made for long-distance walking, and her feet had been killing her by the time they got back to his truck. The time together more than made up for her aching toes.

During the trip home, he'd continued on a theme he'd discussed earlier when he asked if she'd thought about having a family. She'd had to consider her reply.

"Of course I've thought about it," she'd finally said. "What woman hasn't? But after two engagements that never reached the wedding phase, I've started to wonder if it's meant to be for me."

He answered, "You get three strikes for an

out in baseball, and a lot of players have hit home runs after two strikes."

She laughed, but his response got her thinking, and maybe opened a small door in her mind that had been stuck closed. One she hesitated to open any wider. No telling what demons lurked on the other side of it.

When they returned to her house, he pulled into her driveway, parked, got out, and came around to her side to help her down from the truck. He escorted her to her front door.

"I've enjoyed tonight more than I've enjoyed anything in a long time," he said. Then he leaned down and kissed her on the mouth. He kept it brief and light. So brief it ended before she could react. But the sweetness and warmth of it sizzled into her body and seared into her brain.

The memory stayed with her for a long time, and she had a hard time getting to sleep that night.

Once up and running the next day, though, she called Mary Jo Ryder before she left for work and asked if they could meet for coffee that morning. Mary Jo agreed, though she sounded a bit puzzled when Barbara said she had something she needed to discuss privately.

Barbara had to run the regular Monday morning staff meeting at the bank before they opened. As usual Danny couldn't be there since he had classes in the morning, but Tracey and Sheila showed up on time and Cindy blew in five minutes late. Margie came in right after Cindy, apologizing profusely, and saying she'd gotten stuck behind a car stalled at a traffic light. As Margie sat, bright red flashed from the sole of one of her shoes and Barbara wondered if something was stuck there.

She forgot about it, though, as they dove into the nuts and bolts of banking. There were no significant new issues to review, but she did go over again all the warnings about being wary of phishing emails and being careful about their transactions. In light of the fraudulent check they'd had come to light the previous week, she reminded them to be extra vigilant.

Cindy's expression throughout the meeting concerned her. The woman tried to repress a smug smile but didn't quite manage it. Had she already gone to Mary Jo with her complaint about the missing money? Was something already in progress that Barbara didn't know about?

Once the meeting ended and the bank opened, Barbara retreated to her office and closed the door. The call to the mortgage holder of Ruth Freeman's loan took a few minutes to get through to the right person. Barbara identified herself as the manager of the Willow Ridge branch of State Branch Bank, but then made clear she was calling in a personal capacity as a friend of the family. She explained the situation to the man in charge of collections, including the fact that the rest of the family had just learned of the situation and wanted to take care of getting the loan back on track.

She had no trouble talking him into a week's extension on the deadline with a promise that she knew they were serious about repaying, a promise she very much hoped she wouldn't have cause to regret. She had no money riding on it but a lot of credibility.

He was less inclined to grant her request that they be allowed to repay the backlog in installments. "The loan is already in question," he reminded her.

"I know, and I understand your concerns," Barbara answered. "But this is an unusual situation. The family really want to take care of this, but they've had no warning and no time to prepare. They literally just found out about the problem. And they're not wealthy. They've had no time to figure out where they can get the funds to take care of it. They have assets, but they're not particularly liquid. With some time, they can turn some of those into cash to handle the mortgage.

The man finally conceded that if they could come up with half of the loan overdue amount as well as the current payment due in two weeks, that he'd give them another month for the other half. "I'm stretching my authority here," he warned her. "Going out on a limb. Please don't saw it off under me."

"Thank you for that. If they can't pay half of the overdue amount plus the current payment by the fifteenth, I'll let you know as soon as possible so you can take it from there. But I'm sure they can manage that."

She ended the call and debated contacting Chris right away to let him know. But she'd be seeing him later that afternoon. Passing on the information could wait until then.

At ten, she grabbed her purse and warned Cindy she'd be taking an extended coffee break in lieu of a longer lunch time. She walked the few blocks to Latte Da. Millie waved from behind the counter as she entered and asked, "What will it be for you this morning?"

Georgia, Millie's niece and assistant, emerged from the back room with a tray of pastries that smelled delectably of lemon and cream.

"Can I have one of those?" she asked.

"I'm trying a new recipe for Madeleines. You get to do the taste test." Georgia was also a member of the Hopeless Romantics Book Club. She set the tray down and handed over a pastry wrapped in waxed paper.

Barbara took a bite and almost groaned out loud. "Did I die and go to heaven? That's exquisite."

Georgia's smile was an additional reward. Her expression frequently showed a trace of sadness, but not right then. "Glad to hear they're acceptable."

"Oh, so much more than that." Barbara gave her coffee order to Millie and reluctantly turned down an offer of a second pastry. She joined Mary Jo, who already sat at a table near the back with a cup of hot, steaming liquid that smelled like hot chocolate or mocha.

Mary Jo's greeting was friendly and curious, unshadowed by suspicion or doubt, so maybe Cindy hadn't told her about the shortages. They discussed general things about preparation for the Festival at first. Mary Jo had been running the event for years, so she had it all pretty well under control except for a few last-minute issues that always crept in. But even those, she was prepared for.

Millie brought Barbara's coffee, halting the

conversation for a moment. After she'd left Mary Jo asked, "What's up?"

Barbara took a deep breath and told her what had happened after the committee meeting on Saturday. Her stomach fluttered and pulse picked up as she admitted that while she was certain she'd handed over the money, she had no way to prove it. Her mouth got dry and she almost choked on her first sip of coffee.

Mary Jo listened, then pulled a notebook from her purse and began asking her for specifics of how she'd tracked the payments, when she'd handed over registrations and money to Cindy, and what exactly Cindy had said about the missing cash and check. The woman jotted down her answers, scribbling quickly. Barbara's nerves stretched. She felt as though she dug a deeper hole with each word.

After she finished, Mary Jo sat for a few minutes, tapping the notebook with the pen. Then she smiled and said, "Thank you." Before Barbara could recover sufficiently from her astonishment to say anything more, Mary Jo asked, "Does anyone else know about this?"

Another sip of coffee helped restore her power of speech. "Well, Cindy does, of course. And Chris Harper. I wasn't sure what to do when Cindy confronted me about the payments, so I told Chris and asked him for suggestions about how to handle it. He said I should tell you."

She smiled wryly. "Right. I heard you and he were...interested in each other."

"We're friends, helping each other out with a couple of problems."

Mary Jo raised an eyebrow and shrugged.

"Okay. Not my business. But Chris Harper is a good man. I'm glad we have him back in Willow Ridge." She finished up the dregs of the liquid in her cup. "In any case, thank you for bringing this to my attention, and please try not to worry about it too much. Just because you weren't born and raised in Willow Ridge doesn't mean no one will believe you. I can't say anymore...yet, but you should know that this is helpful. We'll get to the bottom of it."

She pulled out her wallet and left a five-dollar bill on the table. "I'm sorry, I need to run, but I'm happy you told me about this. And don't worry. You'll be fine."

CHAPTER 12

Barbara finished her coffee after the other woman had left, wondering what was going on. Did they already have suspicions about Cindy? That left her in a bit of a bind, since Cindy worked for her. Sheila had warned her, though, that Cindy didn't just get mad when she was jealous. Was this part of a bigger plot of some sort?

She put most of that aside when she got back to the bank. Since she planned to leave early, there was plenty of work to take care of. Nothing else disrupted the rhythm of the day, and at three-thirty she shut down her computer, put away all the papers she worked on, and headed out to the animal shelter.

Her stomach churned with nerves as she exited the car. She reminded herself that she'd only agreed to foster Mookie until he could find a forever home. No commitment beyond that.

A young man smiled at her from behind the desk when she entered. "Hey, I'm Daniel. Are you Ms. Wilton?" he asked, standing, and holding out a hand to shake.

She took it and said, "Barbara Wilton. I'm here to pick up a dog?"

"Mookie?" His smile broadened. "You're going to enjoy him. He's a good-natured fellow." He reached for a phone on the desk and told someone to bring Mookie to the front. "We have some things for you."

He pointed to the side of the room, where a crate, a bag of food, and another box stood. "Have you ever fostered before?"

"I've never had a dog at all," she admitted. "I have no idea what I'm doing."

His smile barely wavered. "It's not hard. Dogs are good at telling you what they need, and, honestly, it's pretty basic. Food, water, exercise, and love. Those are the most important things. But we've put together a folder for you. It should cover everything you need to know."

Before he could hand it to her, though, a door from the back opened, allowing a cacophony of barks, squeaks, and the tap of claws on cement to drift through. The noise accompanied the entrance of Mookie, held on a leash by Nancy. Barbara almost didn't recognize the dog. He'd been bathed, fed, and apparently fixed, since he wore a plastic cone around his neck to prevent him from licking or biting himself.

"How long will he have to wear the cone?" she asked.

Daniel grimaced. "Generally about ten days. I know; it's a buzzkill, but we don't want him messing with the stitches."

Mookie walked sedately but steadily toward Barbara, stopping when he was right in front of her and letting out a soft "woof." His tail wagged like a runaway metronome.

"He's happy to see you," Nancy said. "Hold out your hand and let him sniff it. He probably remembers you from Saturday."

She put her hand out tentatively. Since the dog didn't seem inclined to snap at it, she held it steady while he sniffed. Then he stuck out his tongue and licked her palm.

"He likes you," Nancy said.

"Or he likes the remnants of the ham sandwich I had for lunch."

"Also possible," she admitted, laughing.

Mookie nosed around her, then moved to her side and leaned slightly against her legs. And with that, Barbara was hooked. She patted the top of his head, brushing fur that looked fluffy and clean. The softness of it comforted her. He already appeared happier and healthier than he had the other day, despite his recent surgery.

Daniel handed her the folder. "This should tell you pretty much all you need to know, but do you have any questions you'd like to ask now about taking care of him?"

Did she have questions. For the next forty minutes Nancy and Daniel told her about caring for his incision, what to watch for, how to feed him and how much, how to put on his harness, things she should avoid letting him have, the schedule for his medicines and how long he'd need them, and other things she might want to buy for him.

Finally Daniel said, "I'd suggest that you go right to the Pet Center and get him food and water bowls, a big box of treats, and let him pick out a toy or two as well."

Daniel and Nancy helped her load the crate and other supplies into the back of her car and then they used a treat to induce Mookie to jump into the crate.

Taking their advice, she stopped by the Pet Center. That meant putting the harness and leash on Mookie so she could take him inside with her. Her unfamiliarity with the process ensured it took a while to get him ready to go, but he happily jumped out of the car and walked sedately beside her into the store. Once inside, he grew excited and tried to pull on the leash toward a counter of treats, but she told him to stop. To her complete astonishment, he did, sitting suddenly and staring up her, tail wagging a mile a minute.

"Okay, then. Smart doggie. Let's go look for bowls, then treats." She found the bowls and stowed a couple in the cart, then led him to the rows of treats on the next aisle. "What do you like, Mookie?" she asked. She held out several containers of variously flavored dog snacks. He sniffed each, then finally gave an approving woof when she offered up a box of chicken flavored biscuits. "Right. Now a couple of toys."

Those were two aisles over and he wasn't much help in choosing until she picked up an elaborate braided rope creation with fuzzy ends and bells woven into it. Mookie took one end in his mouth and started pulling on it while she held the other. She let go and he continued to shake it. "I guess that's a winner." She picked up a slingshot-looking thing that launched tennis balls, several of which were included in an attached bag. "All dogs like chasing balls, don't they?"

As if he knew the question was directed at him, Mookie gave her an expression that came close to being a silly grin. Then he turned and sniffed along the bins of toys until he came to one that held small stuffed animals. He gently grabbed one in his teeth and brought it to her. Barbara laughed. "Got it."

He went to get another, but she stopped him by tugging on the leash. "Hey, let's don't kill my budget entirely. I think we have plenty."

Another, much smaller dog appeared at the end of the aisle, distracting Mookie from the toys. He went to meet the other canine, who growled and showed his teeth. Mookie froze until the other dog's owner pulled in the leash and moved the growler aside to let them pass.

Barbara checked out and took Mookie out to the car. He balked at getting back in the crate until she tossed two of the new toys in. Then he hopped up and settled in for a good chew while she drove home.

She was still getting Mookie into his harness to take him inside when Chris Harper's truck pulled into the driveway and stopped behind her car.

"Just in time," she told him as he got out. "I'm about to introduce Mookie to the house. Come on along."

She didn't want to admit to being nervous about how the dog would react. Would he take one look and decide to head back to the car? Tear around and trash the place? Neither seemed likely, but what did she know?

That wasn't the only thing she was nervous about. Chris Harper in jeans and tee shirt, his streaky light-brown hair tussled, wearing a smile that showed his dimples, was doing things to her anatomy. Her heart raced and blood fizzed. Dang, she was getting in deep.

She unlocked the door and pushed it open, inviting man and dog to enter. At least she'd straightened up some this morning. Not that she was trying to impress anyone. Not much.

Mookie wandered into the living room and began to sniff around. When he started to lift a rear leg, Chris stood in front of him and said, sternly, "No. Uh, uh. No marking territory inside. No."

The dog lowered his leg and his muzzle and whimpered. Chris patted his head. "Good dog." He looked to her. "Treat, please. You want to reward him for doing as you tell him."

She opened the box and offered him a biscuit. He crunched it up quickly.

"Next time he tries to do that, you should be the one to tell him no," Chris warned her. "You have to establish who's the boss, so don't be wimpy about it. It should only take a couple of times before he understands that he can't go indoors."

Chris went out to retrieve the crate and other supplies from her car while she took off the leash and harness. Mookie explored the rest of the house, poking his nose in various corners and sniffing. He didn't try to raise his leg again.

She had Chris put the crate and pillow in her bedroom. "The shelter people suggested I let him sleep in the crate. I don't care to share my bed with him."

She set up the food and water bowls in a corner of the kitchen and filled each. Mookie was out of the room but heard the rattle of kibble going into the bowl and raced in. Barbara dropped in one of the pills he was supposed to get. The dog gobbled up the food like he hadn't eaten in a week and might never get anymore. The pill disappeared somewhere along the line. She laughed watching him.

Once he was done, he looked around and went to the glass sliding door that let out to the back yard.

"Good idea to let him out now," Chris said. "He might have business to do."

"Business to—oh, *that* kind of business."

"Right."

Mookie raced outside, circled the fenced area, a sizeable bit of land with a few trees and a couple of long-neglected remnants of flower gardens, sniffing and checking things out. Then he chose a far corner to squat.

"Good dog," Chris said, when Mookie returned. The animal vibrated with excitement, the wriggling growing more pronounced when he saw Chris holding a tennis ball. Chris tossed it gently and Mookie took off after it, brought it back, and set it down at Chris's feet. "He's played this game before," Chris noted as he threw the ball again, sending it sailing all the way to the far fence this time.

"It's good for him to get this exercise. By the way, if you want to leave him outside during the day, I don't see that's a problem. The fence is too high for him to jump and the trees and covered porch offer some shade. Be sure he has clean water available, and he'll be fine."

He tossed the ball a few more times, until the dog started to slow down when he chased it. "I think he's getting tired."

"And I'm getting hungry. I have some tomato sauce with meatballs that I took out of the freezer this morning. I just need to throw some spaghetti in a pot and salad in a bowl and it's ready. Want to join me?"

He hesitated for a moment and she worried that she was pushing things with dinner.

CHAPTER 13

Chris was thrilled by the offer, but paused for a moment before responding, trying to recall if he had any other commitments.

"Sure. Mom's out with her friends tonight. She probably left me something, but it'll keep until tomorrow. What can I do to help?"

"Get the salad. There's a bag of greens in the fridge, a couple of tomatoes, and some carrots you can grate or chop."

He got to work on that while she heated water for the pasta and put the sauce in a pan. They talked mostly about Mookie and his care while they fixed the meal. The dog in question sat nearby and looked mournful.

"You might want to get a baby gate to keep him out of the kitchen," Chris suggested."

"Good idea." Barbara used a treat to lure Mookie into his crate so they could eat in peace.

"This is great," Chris said, once they'd taken the edge off their hunger.

"It's pretty simple."

"Simple but delicious." He set down his fork to take a drink. "By the way, my mom sat down with Aunt Ruth, and they went over a bunch of things. I thought Mom handled it well. She told Ruth she wanted to talk about her own situation and how she didn't think she could handle the house by herself once I moved out and wondered how Ruth felt about her own place. Ruth was apparently having one of her better days. Mom said she seemed sharp but was aware that she might be losing track and forgetting things. They talked for a long time and covered a lot of ground. Mom did verify that Aunt Ruth has a will. Ruth showed her where it was and even let her read it. Mom shared a copy of hers with Ruth, too, so they each knew where they stood. The will basically leaves some of Sherm's more valuable things to his nieces and nephews, but the house goes to me and any residual estate to my mom and then to me. So we're covered there. The only thing Mom couldn't do was assess Ruth's cash situation."

"Still, that's a lot of progress."

"There's more. This isn't so definite, but Mom did broach the idea of their moving some place together. It might be Ruth's place or it might be a senior living place. They didn't make any actual plans, but Ruth is considering the idea. I'm guessing Mom will eventually convince her they should stay in her house, for now, at least, but that's probably as much progress as possible right this minute."

"I expect it is. I assume that means you're going to go ahead with plans to try to rescue the house from foreclosure." Barbara took a long drink from her water glass before she told him what she'd learned from her call to the mortgage holder and the concessions she'd gotten.

He looked thrilled by her news. "That's helpful. So we'll need to come up with five thousand by the fifteenth of the month?" He forked up the last bit of spaghetti on his plate and chewed. They might be able to pull that off. "I think we can do that. I just got paid and can use some of my paycheck. I've been saving more since I've been living with mom. And Mom's social security comes through next week, too."

"What will you use to pay your other bills?"

"We'll work it out."

"But you'll get yourself in other trouble," Barbara protested.

"We'll manage." He made the words sound as final as he could. She got the message, nodded, and asked a couple more questions about caring for the dog.

After they'd finished and cleaned up, they took Mookie into the yard again and let him run around. The light was starting to fade. They sat at the table on her back patio to watch him and eat the bowls of ice cream Barbara brought out for dessert.

"With the Festival being tomorrow I'm guessing you're going to have a really busy day," Barbara said once they'd finished.

He'd been trying not to think about it too much. Hopefully there wouldn't be any real trouble. When Chris had consulted with him, Will had warned that there were usually some minor arguments and misunderstandings, especially if the day was especially hot. Tempers flared in the heat and crowds. "I'm expecting so, though I'm hoping it will mainly involve traffic control. What will you be doing?"

"I don't have too many official duties. The bank is co-sponsoring one of the Veteran's groups' floats, so I'll need to check on that. Our Little League team is joining them, but I begged off being on the float itself. I volunteered to man one of the ticket booths for a couple of hours in the afternoon and again in the evening."

"You'll stay busy, I'm betting," he said. "It looks like we're going to get a small break from the weather. Temperatures in the mid-eighties. That's not too bad. It's often a lot hotter than that. Hopefully we won't have too many people passing out from heat."

"I hope not. I was thinking about taking Mookie with me."

He squinted out into the yard. Twilight had deepened to where they could barely see the dog nosing around in the shrubbery. "Probably not a good idea. He's already under some stress, having just had surgery and adapting to a new home. It's a big transition. Plus, you don't know how he reacts to crowds of people."

"I guess you're right. I'll leave him out in the yard. I'd planned to come back here a couple of times to rest and eat, so I'll check on him then."

"Probably a better plan." Chris stood and said, "I ought to get going. We'll both have long days tomorrow. You going to be okay with Mookie?"

The dog recognized his name and came trotting back to nudge Chris, who gave him a good scratch behind the ears.

"I think we'll manage. I hope."

"You'll do fine."

She escorted him to the door.

"I keep my phone close by," he said as they stood in the open doorway. "Call me if there's an emergency."

She looked up at him, staring into his eyes. "I will."

He couldn't help himself. She was too tempting, looking at him that way, like he hung the moon. He leaned down to kiss her. He meant it to be another brief peck, thanks and interest, nothing more serious. Other instincts took over. She was warm, and sweet, and tasted delicious. He wanted more. A lot more.

The kiss went on for a while and might have continued even longer, but Mookie saw an opportunity and tried to squeeze past them out to the front yard. Barbara jumped as the dog pushed against her and grabbed for his collar, breaking the kiss. Once she had firm hold, she looked up at him, and said, "I'm sorry."

Even with the light behind her, he could see the high color in her cheeks and sparkle in her eye. He put a finger on her lips. "Not sure what you're apologizing for, but I hope it's just that the dog interrupted us."

"Yes. Of course." She sounded bemused.

"Good. Good night, then. Hope I'll have a chance to say hello tomorrow." He turned and walked to his truck. She still stood in the doorway, holding onto the dog, watching him with that same stunned look, as he got in and reversed down her driveway. When he turned onto the road, she went back inside and closed the door.

The next morning started early. His alarm went off at four-thirty, and first light had barely sprouted on the horizon when he joined the crew downtown. The barriers that shielded the parade route had been set out the evening before, but they added more of them to cut off all traffic routes into town and put up signs pointing to the designated parking areas. The stand-by ambulance arrived, and he sent it on to its assigned place.

Then the floats, bands, and groups that would form the parade began to gather, and he spent the next hour directing them into place. He and Barbara crossed paths briefly when he signaled the float with veterans and Little Leaguers to take its place. They smiled at each other but had no time or opportunity for more.

Once all the floats were launched, he walked the parade route, staying behind the crowds that lined the curbs and edges of sidewalks, watching for any sign of trouble. The worst that happened was a stray toddler racing toward him, apparently unattended. He stopped the child by moving into its path and leaning down to put a hand on his shoulder. "Hey sport," he said, "where are you off to in such a hurry?"

The surprised child looked up to him, and a sticky piece of candy dropped out of his mouth as he stared. Moments later a breathless father chugged up and stopped. "There you are." He gave Chris a sheepish grin. "I swear I need a leash for this one. I turned to answer his brother's question and—poof—he was gone."

"You have your hands full," Chris agreed as the man took the child's hand. "Enjoy the day." The man nodded and led the toddler back to where two other boys watched a marching band perform.

Chris continued the walk to the end of the parade route, where he shortly became embroiled in trying to sort out a traffic tangle of floats caused when one veered too far to one side and the trailer that held the back part of the float slid the other way, blocking the lane.

An hour later, they finally had the jam cleared; most of the floats had driven off; the marching bands returned to their busses; motorcycles and bikes had ridden away; and the area was mostly free of traffic. He had time for a quick trip home to get a bite to eat and pack a couple more sandwiches for later.

The afternoon passed in a blur of wandering around the festival grounds being sure everything remained under control. The day was hot but not as bad as it could've been. He had a few calls to intervene in juvenile disagreements and to help out when a stove malfunctioned in one of the food booths, sparking fears of a fire that fortunately didn't develop.

He stopped by the booth where Barbara was selling the tickets that people used to buy snacks from some of the vendors, play the various games, and be entered into raffles for prizes. He arrived at a relatively quiet moment.

"You look like a man who could use some water." She reached down and pulled a bottle out of a cooler and handed it to him.

He hadn't realized how dry he'd gotten. He downed half the contents in one long pull. "I think you saved my life," he said, holding the bottle against his face. "I needed that." At her smile, he asked, "How did Mookie do overnight?"

"He was great. I put him in the crate, and he slept all the way through." She laughed as she added, "He was really ready to get out this morning, though. Almost crashed through the back door, he was so eager."

"Glad it worked out okay."

"So far so good."

While they were talking Cindy approached the booth. She gave Barbara a dark look but smiled at him. "Collecting the cash," she explained. "We don't like leaving too much in the booths."

"Makes sense," he agreed. "You need to be careful yourself when you're carrying it."

"I try to be. Of course, if you want to escort me back to headquarters, I'd certainly be grateful."

Idiot, he told himself. He'd set himself up for that. He noticed Barbara carefully counted out the cash, slid it into one of a stack of envelopes she'd brought, sealed it, and wrote the booth and time on the front along with the amount. She flipped it and wrote the amount on the back again, across the seal. Smart woman.

Barbara gave him a wry grin as he finished off the water and went with Cindy to see her and the money safely back to wherever they were storing it. He tried hard to be civil, though the woman's chatter about the heat and the difficulties of organizing the festival and all the problems she'd had rubbed on his nerves. They had to collect money from the other two booths before taking it back to the conference room at City Hall that served as command central for the organization. The people at the other booths didn't package the cash they handed over as Barbara had. They told Cindy the amount they'd given her, and she recorded it in a notebook. He wondered if it would all be in the Festival pot at the end of the day.

He escaped as quickly as he could. The rest of the afternoon and evening were spent patrolling, dealing with a few more squabbles, two minor collisions in the parking area, a stray cat stealing food from a booth, and one fight between a pair of drunk older men.

He didn't see Barbara again until near twilight, when he came across her as she walked to her car. She looked hot and tired but greeted him with a smile that turned wry when she said, "You look beat. It's been a long day. How soon do you get to leave?"

"Probably another hour or so. It's winding down now."

"I'm looking forward to getting to bed soon. But I have to take care of Mookie first."

"Dogs are extra responsibility."

"I know. But..." She hesitated before continuing. "I went home for a quick lunch, and he was so happy to see me. He came running up, tail wagging and ears flapping and wanted me to play with him for a bit. He had food and water, so it wasn't that he really needed anything. He just wanted my companionship."

"And now you understand why people get so attached to their pets. Especially dogs."

"I do." She sighed.

"Mixed emotions about it?" he asked.

"Definitely.

He put an around her shoulders and squeezed. "When the time comes, you'll know what to do."

CHAPTER 14

Barbara had to drag herself out of bed to go to work the next morning. Mookie was awake and making low, whining sounds that likely meant he needed to get outdoors quickly. She threw on a robe, let him out of the crate, and ran with him to the back door. He made a beeline for a shrub near the back of the yard.

She left the door open while she started coffee brewing and filled his food and water bowls.

He was happily crunching Kibble when she went to shower and dress for the day.

The morning started normally, though several of her employees dragged. Cindy had dark circles under her eyes. Sheila had brought her two kids to the festival the day before and showed some lingering after-effects. Her hair looked less perfect than usual, and her makeup was nowhere near so carefully applied. Barbara doubted she looked all that sparkly herself.

The day's first challenge showed up mid-morning, when Mrs. Percy called to say that two more bad checks had been submitted against the account. Both had been returned, unpaid.

She called Chris to report them while she downloaded what information was available, including digital copies of both checks. One check had been written at a WalMart for two hundred and twenty dollars. The second was inscribed to one Vincent Grellar and deposited to an account in that name for almost three thousand dollars. The account in question was with a different bank, and the deposit made through a branch in Savannah.

That much she could tell from the check itself. Any other information about the account would have to come from the other bank. She couldn't get it. Chris could, though, with a warrant. It might be the break they needed.

Chris sounded distracted when she finally got through to him. He was in the midst of something but promised to drop by the bank in an hour or so.

Barbara did her best to keep busy, not wanting to admit how much she looked forward to seeing him and how impatient she grew when an hour went by without his appearance. He showed up thirty minutes later, apologized, but said only, "Got something going that we needed to nail down before I could get away."

She gave him the print-outs of the two checks and explained what the endorsements on the deposited one meant. He studied both. "It may take us a few days to get the information about Vincent Grellar from the bank, but this could be the breakthrough we needed."

"I hope so," she said. "This doesn't look good

for the bank. Or any of us working here."

"No. It doesn't look good for the sheriff's department, either, if we can't resolve it." He flashed a quick smile that disappeared into a worried frown. "We'll get him. Or her. Whoever is doing it."

Watching him, she realized that something else was on his mind, something that made even the check problem secondary. "Something's bothering you," she said.

He'd clenched a fist on the arm of the chair. He noticed and deliberately relaxed it. "It's not something I can talk about right now. You'll know soon enough." He gathered the papers. "I'd better go. Got things to do."

"Okay." She stood when he did. "Thank you for the help."

He nodded to her, then to the others in the office as he left. Barbara watched him go, wondering what was on his mind. At quarter to four, Cindy popped into her office to say she had a meeting with the Festival Committee leaders to go over the finances. The smirk playing around her lips told Barbara that she planned to note, maybe even emphasize, the shortages she claimed in the paperwork Barbara gave her. Barbara reminded herself of Mary Jo's assurance that she'd be all right. That could change, though, depending on how Cindy presented things. She sighed and said, "Okay."

She had other things to worry about. Email had begun to pile up, and a couple of reports were due. None of them caused the same level of concern, though, as her worry about those shortages on the booth registrations.

At four-forty she received a call from Mary Jo Ryder, representing the Festival Committee, asking her to come and talk with them. Right away, if at all possible.

She warned Mary Jo she couldn't leave until five when they closed the bank since Cindy was already gone but promised she'd be over right after that.

The nervous flutters in her tummy erupted into full-scale butterfly gymnastics as she drove the short distance downtown and parked in the nearest lot to the town hall.

Whoever was in charge of clean-up after the Festival had done a terrific job, she noted while walking from the parking area to the building. Although the red, white, and blue bunting had been left in place, no speck of litter remained to tarnish the streets or sidewalks. The grass on the town green looked a bit the worse for wear, but July Georgia heat meant it had been brown and struggling even before the crowd trampled it into the dusty soil the previous day.

Four people sat in the conference room when she arrived. They all glanced up as she said hello and slid into an empty chair. Mary Jo Ryder offered a nod and a tight smile; Ellie McMillan, the vice-chair of the committee wore a serious expression, as did Cindy. Chris Harper, who sat at the far end, facing Mary Jo, looked stern.

The butterflies began to dance in her gut again. All the signs pointed to trouble.

Mary Jo said, "First of all, Barbara, thank you for coming on such short notice." The words were cordial, the tone mostly welcoming, but that turned harsher and more serious as she continued. "We have a problem we hope you can help us with."

"I'm happy to do whatever I can." She knew what the problem was. But what kind of solution were they looking for?

Ellie spoke next. "When we summed up all the recorded income from the Festival, we discovered a shortage of several hundred dollars in the actual amount we had." Her tone and expression came across as serious, with an edge of accusation. Barbara looked around. Mary Jo's and Chris's expressions hadn't changed. Cindy tried to keep hers under control as well, but the smirk started to emerge again.

"We know that some of that shortage—a good bit, in fact—comes from the booth registration list. A couple of booths had recorded payments, but the actual monies were missing."

The silence that followed was thick with accusation and impatience. "I've already spoken with Mary Jo about that shortage. She knows what the issues are."

Mary Jo just nodded.

Ellie continued. "Another, smaller part of the missing money comes from the receipts at the ticket booths. Specifically, the booth you were manning yesterday afternoon and evening."

"But that's not—" A small gesture from Mary Jo cut her off and Barbara got the message.

Understanding dawned. She struggled to keep her expression neutral as the pieces dropped into place.

Ellie continued. "We compared the list of payments Cindy recorded as she collected them against the cash we had in the box. It came up fifty dollars short. And since yours was in an envelope with the amount marked, we knew that the deficit had to come from there."

Cindy's expression was a study in poor acting. She tried to project serious concern but had a hard time controlling the triumph that wanted to break through. "I'm sure there's some reasonable explanation," she said, the words almost smarmy. "An honest mistake. It was hot and busy, and you probably just miscounted the money."

Barbara gave her a long stare. Now that she understood, she didn't have to work hard to keep her expression level and thoughtful. Cindy colored slightly but still fought a smile.

Barbara looked at each of the others in turn, but addressed the question to Mary Jo and Ellie when she asked, "Was anyone else present when Cindy opened the envelope I gave her?"

Ellie answered, "I don't think so. It was already open when she brought it to me and put all the cash in the box."

"I just opened it and added the cash to the rest," Cindy said.

Barbara waited, but it looked like they were going to let her do this herself. As she opened her mouth to speak, though, Chris took care of it for her.

"There was someone else present when Barbara put the money in the envelope and sealed it," he said, directing his attention to Mary Jo. "I watched her count the money. I even counted it with her in my head. And I watched her write the amount on the envelope. That number matched what she put in."

He turned to look at Cindy.

Heavy, dead silence blanketed the room. Cindy turned red, then the color drained from her face as she absorbed what was happening. "No. That's not right," she finally protested. "It can't be right. It wasn't there."

Barbara waited through a quiet pause before adding, "When I gave you the registrations, the one with the cash was on top. I pointed it out to you. There were other people around at the time. I don't know if anyone else could see it was there, but I imagine at least one of the security cameras caught it."

After another fraught silence Cindy said, "That doesn't make any sense. It must've been a mistake. The money wasn't there when she gave it to me."

Ellie answered. "I do think some mistakes were made, but the evidence suggests it wasn't Barbara making them."

Cindy huffed in a sharp breath and went into full indignation mode. "What are you saying? That I'm to blame for the shortages?"

Ellie stared at her. "You're the only other one who had access to the cash in both transactions."

"You're kidding me!" Cindy banged both fists on the table. "Why are all of you taking her word for it? I've lived here all my life. Are you going to believe her—an outsider who got here a few months ago—or me? I've lived here all my life. You know me. You know who I am. What do any of us know about her?" She pointed a shaky finger at Barbara.

Mary Jo answered quietly. "You're right, Cindy. We do know you. And we know your history. I know that two years ago some money also disappeared mysteriously. Someone else was blamed for it, then, but I didn't really believe the person in question took it. Unfortunately, we couldn't prove anything at the time. But we know that person had upset you. And we know that you have a reputation for getting even with people who cross you. This time we can prove what we suspect. The only real question is what to do about it."

"I can't believe this! I've worked my tail off for this committee for years now, and this is the thanks I get?"

"We do appreciate the work you've done," Mary Jo said. "But I'm afraid it's somewhat tarnished by your actions. Deputy Harper and I have talked about how to handle this, and we're going to give you a choice about how we proceed."

She looked to Chris, who continued. "Since the amount you've taken is less than fifteen hundred dollars, under Georgia law you've committed misdemeanor theft. That can carry a sentence of up to a year in prison and a thousand dollar fine. I have to warn you that the evidence is strong enough to pretty much guarantee you'll be found guilty if it comes to that."

He paused a moment to let his words sink in before continuing. "A court case would require several people here to testify, and most of them would prefer not to, so we're offering an alternative. If you'll sign a statement admitting that you were responsible for the deficits, submit it and your resignation to the committee, replace the missing money from the current ledger, and refrain from discussing any of this publicly in the future, the committee will chalk it all up to an unfortunate mistake and no further legal action will be taken."

Again he gave her a minute to absorb the facts. "The choice is yours."

Cindy had gone from pale to looking greenish, but she wasn't ready to let go of her defiance yet. "You can't do this. My dad is part of the Chamber of Commerce. I work for the bank. You'll never convince anyone of this wild story. All my friends and family will deny it."

Mary Jo spoke, trying to be gentle. "It doesn't matter who your father is or what your family and friends think. What matters is that we have enough evidence to take it to court and prove our case. I don't think you want that to happen."

"This is ridiculous. Absurd." Cindy stood abruptly and pointed at Barbara. "She set me up. She did it deliberately. She's the one you should be threatening with jail."

Chris also stood and said, calmly in the face of Cindy's near hysteria, "Barbara has done nothing. I think you should probably give the situation some thought before you say something you will regret."

Mary Jo added. "We'll give you twenty-four hours to think about it. I truly hope you'll accept our offer to take the legal option off the table. And now, I believe this meeting is at an end."

Barbara looked at the time on her phone. "I need to get home to feed my dog." To Cindy, she added, "You might want to take tomorrow off, to think about this. Talk it over with your family and friends you trust. I won't expect you back at work until Monday."

Cindy stalked out of the room without another word to anyone.

Barbara collected her purse and stood. "Thank you. All of you. For digging for the truth. I can't tell you how grateful I am."

Chris approached. "Do you need me to accompany you to your car? Or home?"

"I don't think so. I don't put it past her to plot some kind of revenge, but I think it will take her a while to come up with it."

"Okay, then. Is it okay if I stop by later this evening to say hello to Mookie?"

"I'm sure he'd be thrilled about it," Barbara answered.

CHAPTER 15

His mother had dinner waiting when Chris arrived home. Over the meal he learned that his mom had talked with Aunt Ruth again. The two women had discussed moving in together somewhere. His mom's house had been offered but discarded quickly based on the lack of space. Neither felt they were quite ready for a senior living place yet, which left moving into Ruth's house as the most realistic option. Her home was not only much larger, it had already been modified to be wheelchair accessible when Uncle Sherm had gotten sick and disabled. A number of other modifications made at the time would help both women cope with growing older.

Chris had no emotional attachment to this house himself. After his father died, and with his blessing, his mom had sold the rambling farmhouse he'd grown up in and bought this smaller, more modern place, closer to town.

"Ruth even admitted she was kind of lonely, living in that place all by herself. But we were both concerned about you and whether you'd want to move in, too," his mother asked. "Of course, Ruth is fine with it, if you want, and there's plenty of space, but we did wonder if you might want to be making your own arrangements sometime soon."

"Are you trying to kick me out, Mom?" he asked.

"What? No, of course not."

"You don't think thirty-two is a bit old for a man to still be living with his mother?"

"Christopher Madison Harper, you know better than that."

He laughed. "You're right, Mom. I do."

"But seriously. If I do move in with Ruth, it would free you up if you wanted to...pursue other options. You know, like the pretty banker you've been seeing? Isn't that where you're planning to go tonight?"

He felt the heat rush to his face. "She needs help training the dog."

"And that's all?"

His mother knew him too well.

"No, it's not all. But there's a major roadblock between us. She doesn't plan to stay in Willow Ridge. Her career is important to her and advancing will mean she'll have to go to a bigger city, eventually."

"Savannah's in commuting distance. In any case, are you sure you want to stay here? I know perfectly well why you came back. But maybe that's not as relevant now?"

"My reasons for coming back were...complicated. More than just concern for you. I needed a change after the divorce." And Willow Ridge welcomed him back, gave him a job that he was enjoying more than he expected to, offered a warm embrace and encouragement from many of the people, and provided surprising comfort in its unhurried pace. Not to mention Barbara Wilton. She figured in that, too.

"I imagine so," she said. "Anyway, I talked to Scott Meyers about getting an appraisal for the house. He'll be coming out on Monday."

"Okay. I'm not sure what I'll do. I need to give it some thought."

"Of course."

He couldn't stop thinking about it while he helped clean up after dinner. His thoughts drifted to having his own place in Willow Ridge. A house like this or Barbara's, with room for a family and a nice yard for a dog. Six months ago, a thought like that would have rubbed the open wound of his failed marriage. Now the fantasy beckoned him to indulge. Except he could only envision sharing the house and family with one particular woman. One who didn't want to stay there.

He hung up the towel and headed for Barbara's place.

She opened the door when he knocked and invited him in. He refused offers of coffee, lemonade, or soda, but accepted a beer. She poured herself a glass of lemonade and they took the drinks outside to the patio in back. Mookie chewed on a stick near the gate to the driveway but came running to greet them when they stepped out the door. He nosed up to Chris right away, begging to be petted.

He fussed over the dog for a couple of minutes, then sat with Barbara at the table.

"Have you recovered from this afternoon?"

he asked.

"Mostly. I'm relieved to be off the hook for shorting the money. But there's also… This is going to be so awkward. I have to work with Cindy. I'm hoping she got the message and doesn't come in tomorrow, but it's going to be difficult whenever she does come back. She's already tried to undermine me in subtle, and sometimes not-so-subtle, ways. This will give her even more incentive."

"You'll need to be extra-careful. If she's been undermining you, do you have reason to fire her?"

"I don't know. I'll have to check with some of the higher-ups. Theft of any sort is generally grounds for dismissal, but since her admission, if she makes one, is supposed to remain confidential and there won't be any legal proceedings, I'm not sure."

"Okay." The dog pushed his nose into his hand, distracting them both. "Have you taught him to sit on command yet?"

"No. Should I? How?"

"Yes, you should. He looked at the dog. "Mookie sit," he said, in a firm voice. The dog stared at him. Chris reached for the box of treats and took one out. Holding the biscuit in front of the dog, but pulling it away when Mookie lunged for it, he repeated, "Mookie, sit." He pushed the animal's rear end down until he was sitting, then he gave him the treat. He repeated the request, pushing down, and handing over the biscuit again.

"Now, you do it," he told Barbara. "You're the one he needs to listen to and obey."

"Okay." She got a treat and said, "Sit,

Mookie." He stared at the biscuit in her hand, tail wagging happily. She pushed his hind end down until he was sitting, and she gave him the treat. She did it again and again, until on the fourth time, some bulb lit up in his doggie brain. When she said, "Sit, Mookie," he actually did.

"Good dog!" She handed him the treat.

Chris enjoyed hearing the delight in her voice. "Try it again," he urged.

She told the dog to sit, and he did.

"Good. He's getting the idea."

Barbara did it one more time and the dog sat again. Chris picked up a tennis ball from the concrete nearby, showed it to Mookie, and tossed it to the back of the yard. The dog tore off after it and nosed around in the shrubbery at the far corner until he found it. After bringing it back, he dropped the ball in front of Chris, and rounded the table to sit in front of her. When Barbara reached for another treat, Chris said, "No. He should only get a treat when he sits at your command."

"Got it."

"You should try taking him for walks, so he can learn to walk beside you."

"Maybe tomorrow, after work." Barbara took a long drink of lemonade. "Before the game. Will you be there?"

"Yup. I'm on call, but otherwise I'm on day shift for the next couple of weeks."

"Good."

He finished the beer, and she went in to get him another bottle and refill her lemonade. When she sat again, he said, "By the way, it looks like Mom's going to move in with Aunt

Ruth and sell the house she's in now."

"Is that a good thing? For her?"

"I think so. They can help each other."

"And you? Will you move, too?" she asked.

"Guess I'll have to move somewhere if Mom sells the house."

"Okay. That was a non-answer."

He grinned. "Because I don't know what I'm going to do yet. Maybe it's time to get my own place. They won't actually need me to be living with them, as long as I'm close by. For now, at least."

They sipped drinks for a while in companionable silence as the sun sank below the horizon and twilight deepened to darkness.

"It's incredibly peaceful here," she said, after a while. "I didn't expect that, for some reason. But I feel like that quiet and calm are washing into my soul."

He reached out and took her hand. Light seeped out the door to the kitchen behind her, leaving her face in shadow. The darkness made it easier to say the deeper things. "I know what you mean. I think. I feel like something here is finding those jagged places in my spirit and smoothing out the edges, so it doesn't hurt as much anymore."

Tired out by running around and playing, Mookie settled down at their feet under the table and began to snore lightly. Pale lightning flashed in the distance.

"I didn't know dogs snored," Barbara said. "But then I didn't know a lot of things about dogs. Still don't. But this one is... Well, he's pretty easy to get along with."

"You're going to miss him when he gets

adopted."

She drew in a deep breath and let it out slowly. "I will. It's going to be hard to let him go."

"You can call them any time and tell them you want to adopt him."

"I know. But that's a big step. A big commitment."

He increased the pressure on her hand a little, not enough to hurt, just enough, he hoped, to offer reassurance and support. Words hung on the tip of his tongue. Words that would make explicit the longing he heard underlying her comments, words that would urge her toward making that decision in a way he wanted. But he didn't say anything. She needed to make the choice on her own terms. No matter what he thought he wanted.

The contact of their hands felt like a conduit, communicating needs and desires and hopes between them. At least he experienced it that way. She turned slightly toward him, meeting his gaze. They stared into each other's eyes in the dim light. He was almost sure he saw longing in her eyes and felt it in the way her hand gripped his. Conflict, too, though. He started to lean toward her, need drawing him closer.

A sudden rumble of thunder split the night. Mookie jolted awake under the table and surged to his feet. His cone, and then his head, smashed against the bottom of the table, which rocked and crashed to its side. Her glass and his beer bottle both hit the concrete and smashed. They startled apart, staring at each other in sudden dismay, which gave way to amusement and then concern when Mookie started licking the spilled remnants of the beer, unheeding the broken glass.

She shot up from her seat. "No, Mookie! No!" She grabbed his collar and dragged him away from the spill, careful to avoid stepping on broken glass herself and making sure the dog's paws didn't land on any. He opened the back door for her. She pushed Mookie inside, and he closed it the second she moved out of the way.

They spent the next few minutes setting the table upright and cleaning up broken glass from the patio. She brought a broom and dustpan from inside to sweep the concrete. Chris retrieved a flashlight from his truck, and they scanned the ground at the edge of the patio as well as along the concrete surface to be sure they had every sliver. The wind started to pick up as they finished.

Once back inside, Barbara checked Mookie's paws for any bits of glass that might've already stuck in him or clung to his fir. Fortunately, he bore no sign of injury or slivers. She even induced him to open his mouth for a treat so she could check his tongue for blood.

"Foolish dog appears to have had a lucky escape," she said. "Who knew dogs liked beer?"

"Are you sure it wasn't the lemonade?"

"He was licking where the beer in the bottle spilled."

"At least we know he's got good taste." Chris looked at the clock. "I'd better get rolling. We both have to work tomorrow."

She escorted him to the door again and they stopped there before she opened it.

"How about if I come here after work

tomorrow? I'll stop at home to change and pick up my team shirt and cleats. Maybe stop and get some pizza too? We can have dinner and walk the dog before we head out to the game."

"That sounds great," she said.

"Barbara..." He let it trail off. Instead he put a hand on the side of her head and ran his fingers through her sleek hair. Then he leaned down and kissed her. As before, he meant it to be brief. And as before his will power failed when her soft, sweet lips moved under his. Instead of pulling back, he deepened the kiss, and she responded, with enthusiasm. So much enthusiasm. So much joy. He pulled her closer. He had no idea how long the kiss lasted. It could've gone on a lot longer and he wouldn't have cared. Wouldn't have minded at all.

But she ran out of breath and had to pull back, panting, trembling, eyes glazed. She put a hand on his shoulder to steady herself. When she looked him in the eye, everything he wanted to see was there.

But did she know it?

He gave her one more kiss, a quick one this time, and moved back to open the door. "I'll see you tomorrow," he said. His voice almost cracked in a way it hadn't since he was sixteen.

He got in his truck just as the rain started.

CHAPTER 16

Barbara moved around the house, cleaning up, getting ready for bed, reassuring Mookie that he was a good boy despite the calamity of earlier, and settling him for the night, all in a bemused haze. Chris's kisses did something to her, stirred a need she'd thought dead since the end of her last engagement. Maybe even longer than that. His company and conversation made her feel alive and happy in ways she could barely remember experiencing before.

Looking back now she had to wonder if she'd really loved Craig that much. Certainly she'd thought so at the time. But had she been as into him as she'd been with Gavin? Maybe not. Craig took her out and wined and dined her. He'd been kind and understanding. He'd dazzled her. She'd loved it. His attention made her feel whole again after Gavin's death. But had she loved him? Possibly not. And maybe he finally sensed something amiss or realized he didn't have her whole heart. He still handled the whole thing badly, waiting too long to call things off, but perhaps she'd helped cause the break, on some level, because she'd mistaken the gratitude and relief she felt for love.

She couldn't remember feeling about Craig the way she was starting to feel for Chris. Gavin, yes. They'd been so close. They fulfilled each other in ways neither of them understood. And when he'd died, part of her had been ripped away. The wound had taken years to heal. But now she realized the injury from Craig had damaged her pride more than her heart.

Even so, she didn't want to risk falling in love again. But it might already be too late. Chris Harper had worked his way into her life, her mind, and her heart, almost without her realizing how deeply he'd embedded himself until his residence there was already a fact. She came alive in a new way in his presence, every nerve ending buzzing in anticipation of his words, his gaze, his touch, his kisses.

Barbara hadn't seen it coming, this unexpected love for another man. The emotions crept up on her so quickly, yet so quietly, that he'd planted himself in her heart almost before she knew he was there.

That realization terrified her. And filled her with elation. How was it possible to feel both at the same time?

What if he didn't feel the same? She thought he did. He must. The way he kissed her went beyond any expression of just friendship. But life had sliced him open in ways as brutal as her own wounds. Had he healed enough to be ready for another relationship?

And the Willow Ridge problem. He'd hinted that he intended to stay, at least for a while. And she—? She didn't know, actually. She'd be here for a while, too, anyway. A couple more years, probably. After that? Well, who knew?

On that thought, she fell asleep.

Mercifully, Cindy didn't come to work on Friday and Barbara had a reasonably normal, quiet day. The only interruption in the routine occurred when Chris called to update her on his investigation into the bad checks on the Percys' account and get more information from her.

"I went to Savannah to visit Sam Russell in the nursing home. He's not entirely coherent and his memory's unreliable. But I did get the names of some relatives to track down, mostly from the staff there."

Barbara needed a moment to remember Sam Russell's home had been the address where the questionable checks had been mailed. "Sounds like they might be worth following up with."

"Yeah. It's just going to take some time. I also got the warrant for information on the account opened in the name of Vincent Grellar. It has to be checked by the bank's legal department, but I should have it early next week. Between those two leads, we should resolve this soon."

"Glad to hear it," she said. She hoped he was right. Not clearing it up could cast a shadow over her career for a long time.

He asked for a couple more details about the checks. After she'd given it to him, he said, "Thanks. Oh, did Cindy show up today?"

"No. And I'm just as glad."

"It makes me wonder..." he said. "Given her feelings about you, I think I'll check to see if she has any connection to Sam Russell. Or one

Vincent Grellar. If he exists.”

That gave Barbara pause. “I don’t like to think she’d go that far. Lifting small amounts of money from an organization’s treasury is one thing, but bank fraud is far more serious.”

“I know. We don’t know how far she’d go. It’s worth checking out anyway.”

“Okay. I really hope that doesn’t turn up anything, though.”

“You’re more generous than I think I’d be,” Chris said before they ended the call.

At the end of the day, she locked up and set the alarms as usual, then headed home to change clothes and feed Mookie.

Chris knocked on her door a little after six, holding a pizza box. Because the ballgame was at seven-thirty, they ate quickly and took the dog for a short walk.

Mookie cooperated when she put on his harness and attached the leash. As though he sensed a new adventure in the offing, his tail wagged nonstop. When she opened the door for them to head out, he dove through enthusiastically and pulled her forward in his excitement to explore the world.

They walked up the road for a half mile or so, though Mookie stopped every hundred feet to sniff at something, and frequently raised his leg.

“I read up about dog behavior on the internet,” she told Chris as they enjoyed the casual stroll in the fading heat of the day. “I gather he’s marking his territory?”

“That seems to be general idea,” he answered.

Mookie spotted a squirrel and tried to take

off after it, nearly dragging Barbara off her feet. Chris wound an arm around her shoulders to steady her while she pulled the leash back. The dog turned and gave her an offended look once she drawn him back to her side. "Sit, Mookie," she said.

He gave a longing look back to where the squirrel had run up a tree, then with an almost audible doggy sigh, he sat.

"Good dog!" she gave him a treat.

For the rest of the walk, he continued to explore all the interesting aromas along the way and put his stamp of ownership on any place that needed it. But he didn't pull away again.

When they returned home, she let him loose in the back yard while she changed into her team jersey for the game. Chris took his into her bathroom.

They drove to the ballpark in his truck. As the sun retreated toward the horizon, the day's heat moderated and a gentle breeze blew, making conditions almost pleasant.

She greeted the players she recognized as she settled her equipment on a bench near the dugout. Tyler came over and said, "I've been practicing what you told me about reach toward home plate after I throw, and I think it's really making a difference."

Carl approached and said, "Glad to hear it. Jeff's knee is bothering him and he's not sure how long he can go." Jeff was their regular pitcher. "Should warn all of you. The guys we're facing today are at the top of the league. Undefeated. So we've got quite the challenge ahead." He turned to Barbara. "Tom's out, so I'm moving Tony to his position in center field.

You're on second base today."

A few of the players grumbled about her starting there, including the catcher, Jarrod, who sneered. "Think you can handle a throw from home on a steal, Wilton?"

She'd tried ignoring his jibes in the previous game. She was done with that strategy. Time to give it back to him. "If the throw comes to the right place, yes. Think you can put it in the right place?"

"If I can figure out where that is when a girl is getting the ball."

She stared at him and said, "It's the same place whether it's a woman or a man fielding it."

Chris turned to Jarrod, about to say something, but she shook her head, and he backed off.

Nobody on their team had a great game. Jeff gave up five runs in four innings and admitted he wasn't in his best form. Nor did they have much luck against the opposing pitcher. Barbara watched him carefully, trying to read his body language and throwing motion for clues. She couldn't find anything. During one of the breaks between half innings someone mentioned that the man had once pitched professionally for a minor league team.

"I'm not surprised," she said. "He's good."

"And we're not?" Jarrod had overheard her remark.

"How many of us have played professionally?" she asked. "Has anyone on this team played even Low A?"

No one answered.

The rest of the game wasn't much better,

even when Tyler replaced Jeff as pitcher. He only gave up two more runs but none of their players could get more than a few weak ground balls off the other side.

A runner from the other team did try to steal second base in the sixth inning. Seeing him going, Barbara moved over to cover the base. Jarrod's throw went so far over her head, the runner made it home before the center fielder could recover it.

At the end of the inning Jarrod refused to look at her. She toyed with jibing him about the error and decided to forgo the satisfaction. She would stand up to a bully, but she wasn't going to imitate him.

When the game ground to its dreary conclusion, she and Chris said goodnight and piled into his truck. "Man, that was bad," she said, depressed about her own effort. "I struck out three times!"

"So did I." But Chris sounded less discouraged. "We just played a team that was a lot better than us. It happens."

"I suppose so," she admitted. "But I don't like it."

"No one likes losing. But it's part of life. And it's a game. We're supposed to be playing it for the fun of it."

"True, but winning is more fun than losing." She made it more teasing than complaint, recognizing that he was right. Even so, she had to admit to herself that the loss rankled.

He laughed. "We'll do better next week."

"Hope so. It's the last game."

When they arrived at her house, he escorted her to the door and leaned in for a kiss. She loved the way he kissed, the way it made her feel, but this time it was cut short when they heard Mookie barking for attention inside.

They laughed and he said goodnight.

The next morning she had to get up for a Little League game, which thankfully happened with almost no drama. Her kids won a close game by one run, and she took them all to a fast food place up the road and bought them lunch to celebrate. Chris was on duty on Saturday, but he called at four. When he asked if she had any plans for that evening and she admitted she didn't, he suggested dinner and a movie. He offered the choice of a science fiction action movie and a rom-com, both playing at theaters nearby, and he sounded gratified when she chose the super-hero movie.

"I have nothing against a good romantic comedy," she told him later as they drove to the restaurant. "But I've been wanting to see this sci fi movie for a while."

"I don't have anything against romantic comedy either," he said, "As long as it doesn't get too sappy."

They both enjoyed dinner and the movie, though neither felt the film was as good as some of the others in the series. The next day Chris had promised to take his mother shopping in the afternoon after church and dinner. He invited her to join them for the meal and shopping trip, if she wanted. He admitted his mother was eager to meet her.

Barbara recognized that accepting the offer moved their relationship to another level. She acknowledged that their interest in each other was serious and might lead to something lasting. She still didn't know how that could work for them, but she wanted to find out.

She arrived at his home a few minutes early the next day, after driving some distance to a twenty-four-hour supermarket in a neighboring town to get a cheese tray and an arrangement of flowers.

Though Chris told her his mother had some health issues, Barbara wouldn't have guessed on first meeting her. The woman who demanded, "Call me, Dee, please, dear," on being introduced, appeared warm, lively, and dynamic. She invited Barbara in and appeared delighted with the gifts. "How very thoughtful of you," she said. "Come back to the dining room. Let me get a vase for the flowers and I think dinner is ready for us to sit down."

The meal was wonderful. Barbara liked his mother right from the start. The woman was kind, generous, and took a lively interest in a broad range of topics. They discussed sports, movies, books, the town, politics, and her career. They didn't agree on everything but could happily agree to disagree. Dee complimented her on fostering the stray dog, and they discussed how his training was going.

The food was also excellent. Barbara's culinary experience in New England hadn't included fresh-from-the-garden tomatoes and salad greens, Southern-style fried chicken, or biscuits so light they practically floated away. The flavors delighted her, and Dee glowed with pleasure at Barbara's compliments. Afterward, she volunteered to help Chris clean up while his mother got ready for shopping.

They had a grand time at a mall on the

outskirts of Savannah. Actually, Chris might not have enjoyed it much, but he was a good sport while Barbara and Dee explored stores featuring interesting clothes and exciting shoes. They tried on various outfits and laughed at the way some things looked on them. Dee needed a couple of new pairs of jeans, but Barbara found a pretty blouse to go with them that looked great on her and wouldn't break the bank. They also bought her a new pair of walking shoes that Barbara considered stylish and Dee found comfortable.

Chris was surprisingly quiet and thoughtful as they drove back to his mother's house.

"Sorry we put you through that ordeal," Barbara said to him, jokingly, trying to lighten the mood.

But his response was more serious than she expected. "Not an ordeal. It was enlightening."

"What? How?"

"I never thought the two of you would get along so well. You're so…different."

Barbara and Dee looked at each other. It was true, Barbara thought, but…

"We have a lot more in common than you might think," Dee said. "She's a city girl and I'm a country woman. But we both like pretty things, we both like hunting for them, but I think we both recognize that pretty things are nice but they're not the most important things in life. Isn't that so, Barbara?"

She looked into Dee's eyes again and saw so much understanding there. "Yes. Undoubtedly."

A slight smile crawled across Chris's face. "Okay."

Eventually, Chris took her home and said goodnight with another lingering kiss that made her want more and more and more. Only as she started to get ready for bed did she think about the next day and the challenges it would likely bring.

Monday morning came all too quickly. Reluctance dragged her steps as she fed the dog and let him run outside while she got ready for work.

Margie and Cindy were already inside when she arrived, a fact that vaguely alarmed her, though she had no actual idea why. Margie waved at her from her desk behind the teller counter. Cindy looked up and nodded as she walked past.

Barbara locked her purse in the bottom drawer of her desk, then started on the usual morning chores before they opened the doors to admit the public. When she finished those, she returned to her office and turned on the computer to check messages. Her concentration on email was broken when Cindy tapped on the open office door.

"Barbara? Can I talk to you a minute?" She sounded uncharacteristically subdued and tentative.

Barbara swiveled away from the computer to face the woman. "Come in."

Cindy shut the door behind her and took a seat in one of the guest chairs. She wove her fingers together in her lap before she spoke. "I've been doing a lot of thinking and talking to people since last week. A lot of soul searching. And I've realized that what I did was wrong.

Stupid, too." A quick, wry grin appeared and disappeared just as fast. "I signed the paper admitting what I'd done and gave it to Mary Jo. And I need to apologize to you for…for all of it. I have lots of reas—excuses, but none of them are good enough. I realize I'll be lucky if the bank doesn't fire me, but I'd like to try to do better. In my life and in the job here if I get to keep it. I want to do what I can, learn what I need to be a better assistant manager."

Barbara studied her, wondering if she dared trust this new, repentant Cindy. How long would this improved attitude last? But she elected to work with it. "All right. Let's see if we can't begin again." She held out a hand. "I'm Barbara Wilton."

The other woman took her hand and shook it, smiling. "I'm Cindy Martinson, your assistant manager. Someday I'd like to move up to a manager position, but I have a lot to learn first."

"I have a few suggestions."

Tracey knocked on the closed door. She waited for Barbara's nod, then pushed it open, leaned in, and said, "Sorry to interrupt, but we're way backed up at the drive-through."

Cindy rose to go.

"I'll email you links to some online workshops," Barbara said, "And we'll discuss it more later."

Cindy's "Thank you," sounded sincerely grateful.

Customers wandered in and the phone on her desk rang. The day continued, busily but normally until sometime around two. She had a client in her office, filling out paperwork for a short-term loan when the pen she'd handed the man ran out of ink. She opened her top desk drawer to get another one and was surprised to find a small pasteboard folder she didn't remember leaving there.

While the customer signed the forms, she pulled out the folder and opened it. She dropped it on the desk like a hot potato when she realized what it was.

She must've made some sound because the customer looked up and asked, "Is everything all right?"

Barbara choked out an answer that apparently relieved the man, but she was far from all right. The customer left a few minutes later with her promise to get the papers submitted right away and thanks for his business.

Her hands shook, though, as she punched in the number for the sheriff's department.

CHAPTER 17

Chris's Monday had consisted of one frustration after another. Two deputies wanted the same time off next month. Reports that should've been filed on traffic incidents the previous week were missing. And, of course, the insurance companies wanted them right away. His follow-up with potential relatives of Sam Russell had come up empty so far. The magistrate insisted on having every i dotted and t crossed before he'd sign off on the warrant for information on the Vincent Grellar bank account.

Chris wasn't in the best of moods when Barbara's phone call came in. But what she said made him stand up and grab his gear before she'd even hung up the phone.

Business as usual prevailed at the bank when he arrived. Apparently, no one but Barbara knew anything out of the ordinary had occurred. She stood at the door of her office and waved him in. She looked shaken in a way he'd never seen her before. Even when Cindy had accused her of stealing money from the Festival

Committee, she'd been concerned, but not rattled.

The hand that pointed to an item on her desk shook, and her breath came in shallow gasps. "I found it in my desk drawer this afternoon."

He snapped on a pair of latex gloves before he picked up the cardstock folder with the bank's name and logo on the front. Flipping it open revealed three pads of blank checks glued to the paper. The Percys' names and address jumped out at him, along with the check numbers, which were in the seven thousands. A few checks had been removed from the top pad, but the others were intact.

"I have no idea how those got in my desk," she said, her voice shaking.

He'd brought an evidence bag inside with him, so he dropped the book of checks into it and sealed it.

"Tell me how you found it."

She explained about the customer doing paperwork and needing another pen.

"Was that the first time today you've opened that drawer?"

She thought about it for a moment. "Yes, I'm pretty sure it was. I put my purse in the bottom drawer and locked it, and I pulled some forms out of the second drawer earlier, but I didn't need anything from the top drawer until that pen."

He looked at the glass door which stood open. Two sides of the office were also walled with glass. "Is your office locked when you're not in it?" he asked.

"Only at night. During the day it's not only not locked, the door is usually open. People come in all the time to leave things on my desk or get forms if they're out of them."

"Is the top drawer locked?"

"No, I only lock the bottom drawer because my purse is in it."

He nodded, thinking furiously. "So anyone could have put this in your drawer?"

She grew paler. "Anyone who works here. I doubt a customer could come in and leave it in my desk without someone noticing. We're pretty careful about that." She drew a deep raspy breath. "I don't want to think..." She let it trail off.

Several thoughts he didn't want to entertain crossed his mind, but he had to consider them. "Would you come with me to the office to fill out some paperwork and make a statement?" he asked.

"Of course."

Her hands still shook as she retrieved her purse from the bottom drawer. She didn't lock her office door, but she did lean into Cindy's space to warn her she'd be out for a while.

When they got in the car, she said, "I wonder if the cameras might've caught someone going into my office? It almost has to be someone who works there, but I just can't believe it. Unless it was Cindy, but she seemed so sincere this morning when she apologized and all." Her quiet words seemed to reflect her thinking over the situation rather than trying to tell him anything.

But still, he asked, "Cindy apologized?"

She turned to him as though coming out of a fog. "Yes, this morning. Said she was sorry for what she'd done, and she wanted to do better.

Learn to do her job properly, even. She sounded sincere."

"You believed her?"

"Yes. With reservations."

"Okay. Look, Barbara..." He let it hang, trying to formulate the right words for what he needed to say. The silence stretched on too long before he continued. "I'm going to submit the check folder to the lab and take your statement, but then I'm going to have to officially remove myself from this investigation. Will McCormick is about ready to come back to work as sheriff, and I'll turn it over to him. He's a good man, a good sheriff, and fair."

"I don't... Oh. Oh." Pain tightened the words as she added, "I'm now a suspect in the case."

He reached out and clasped a hand over hers. "I don't believe you were responsible. But the circumstance of the checks turning up in your desk automatically makes you a suspect. And because I'm emotionally involved with you, I have to take myself off the case."

"Understood." He could tell she did but didn't like it.

"I'll still do what I can to help and support you. But..." Having to say the words hurt him almost as much as it was going to pain her. "We'll have to stop seeing each other for a while. Until this is cleared up."

"Even if you take yourself off the case?"

"I'm afraid so. It wouldn't look good for the department to have a deputy dating a suspect, no matter how unlikely it is she's guilty."

She turned a weak, wavering smile his way. "Okay. I understand. Thank you for the vote of confidence, at least. I appreciate it. Are you going to…? Will I be arrested?"

"No. Given the circumstances, I don't think we have enough probable cause, especially since you called in the report of those checks yourself. And there are other possible suspects."

"That's a relief. I guess."

"The sheriff is going to want to get fingerprints from all your employees to match what we get off the checkbook."

She closed her eyes for a moment. "We were all fingerprinted when we were hired."

"For background checks? We can get those, but it will take time and paperwork. Easier and quicker if we can ask your employees to voluntarily let us fingerprint them now. We'll want to talk to each of them anyway. I expect Will to ask each employee to come in to the station separately."

She stayed silent for a few minutes.

"We'll get it resolved," he said. "As quickly as we can."

"I hope you're right." She sounded so dejected he wanted to pound the steering wheel in frustration.

At the station, he took her to a conference room where she gave a recorded statement about finding the checks and answered all of his questions. Afterward, he offered to drive her back to the bank, but she declined, saying she'd prefer to walk.

"One more thing," he said as she stood. "Please don't tell anyone at the bank about this. We'll do better questioning them if they don't know about the checks."

"I won't," she said quietly.

He watched her leave and had to fight with himself to keep from following and hugging her again. She looked so depressed.

Once she left, he called Will McCormick. The sheriff answered the phone himself and admitted he was feeling much better and eager to get back to work.

Chris explained the situation.

Will stayed quiet for a moment. "You're sure she's not guilty? We don't know much about her."

"I do. And I'm sure of it. She called in the reports initially and notified us the moment she found those checks. Why would someone who's guilty do that?"

"She's a smart woman. She might have done it to deflect the guilt from herself."

Chris considered that. "She is a smart woman. So smart, in fact, that if she was the guilty party, we would have no idea anything at all out of the ordinary was happening right now."

"That's a good point," Will agreed. "Okay, get someone to line up interviews with each of the employees tomorrow. I'll be there in the morning."

CHAPTER 18

Barbara had to fight a serious case of depression for the rest of the day. Some of her employees at the bank noticed and a couple asked her about it, but she kept the reasons to herself.

Chris assured her they would clear up the fraudulent check case and find the guilty party. But what if they didn't? Even if she weren't arrested, that suspicion could follow her for a long time and ruin her banking career. And if they did arrest her and there was a trial...? She couldn't bear to contemplate that nightmarish scenario.

Would she ever be able to see Chris again, or would they be forever banned by her status as suspect? Would he continue to believe in her if they couldn't find the guilty party? Those fears cut deeply, more deeply than she expected. In a short time he'd become an important part of her life. Not seeing him that evening created sharp disappointment. How could she even think about an end to their relationship?

She kept it together for the rest of the work

day, but when she got home, she sat on the sofa and let the emotion surge. At first she just shook, but after a few minutes the tears started.

Mookie wandered into the living room. As though sensing her disturbed emotions, he walked right up and stuck his head in her lap. The edge of the cone bit into her leg, but she didn't care. She patted his fuzz, and he licked her arm. He jumped up on the sofa where she sat and plopped himself down next to her with his front paws and head on her legs. Barbara took off the cone, leaned down, and buried her face in his fur for a few minutes while letting herself go.

The dog seemed to sense that she needed him. She hadn't yet fed him, but he didn't make any motions toward the kitchen. He rested on her lap, letting her hug him and allowing the fur on his head and neck to absorb her tears, just as his warm body and unquestioning affection absorbed some of her pain.

She'd already pulled herself up out of the depths and started over so many times. How could she do it again? She tried to tell herself that wasn't likely to happen. Chris—or someone—would get to the bottom of it and she'd be cleared. She struggled to believe it. So many things had gone wrong in her life. It had become easier to see that as normal.

Maybe she could figure out who put those checks in her desk herself. She'd promised not to say anything about them, but after the sheriff talked to everyone, they'd all know anyway, and she could ask some questions. Thinking that any of her employees might be responsible made her sick to her stomach, but it was so unlikely anyone outside the bank could have accessed her desk without someone noticing and remarking on it.

She would have to investigate it herself. The anticipation of doing something, anything, about the situation helped. She wiped away the tears and stood. Mookie jumped off the couch, heading for the kitchen. She replaced the cone, fed him, and let him outside while she fixed her own dinner.

Watching television and reading helped distract her for a time, but her thoughts kept drifting back to the problems she faced. Mookie sat with her once he came back in from outside. He stayed closer to her than normal all evening. She never guessed that dogs could sense a person's mood, but clearly Mookie was convinced she needed him nearby. He was right.

The next day felt entirely weird, almost surreal. One by one her employees disappeared for a time, each saying they'd received a call asking them to come to the sheriff's office to discuss a "sensitive issue." Each came back looking sober and some even seemed rattled. They all declined to discuss the matter when others asked about it. Cindy was the last to be called and she looked positively white when she returned at four.

Tuesday evening felt as lonely as the previous one. She took Mookie for a walk and couldn't help remembering the last time when Chris had been with her. Mookie behaved like a perfect gentleman on their stroll, and once again he stayed close to her until bedtime. She wondered if he missed seeing Chris, too.

Cindy was the first to arrive on Wednesday morning. She waited in the parking lot when Barbara pulled in at quarter to eight. Barbara went inside and did the usual sweep while Cindy waited in her car until she got the all-clear sign.

"Can I talk to you?" the other woman asked as soon as they'd reset the alarm and prepared the place to open.

"Sure." Barbara led the way to her office.

"They think I stole those checks," Cindy said the moment she sat down. "They practically came out and said that I put them in your desk drawer to frame you. But I didn't. I swear I didn't. I don't think they believed me, though. I know that after the Festival Committee fiasco people don't trust me as much. And they think I have even more reason to dislike you. But this is different. I've learned my lesson, but they're still suspicious of me. Even when I told them that I'd seen a couple of other people in your office when you weren't there."

"A couple? Who?"

"The thing is I didn't really see anything other than them going in or out. And I don't like to think that anyone I work with would... You know."

"I do. And I don't like to think it either. Who was in here?"

"You know Margie and I were in early Monday, before you got here. I unlocked all the doors. At one point Margie went into your office to get some blank TR-90 forms. I didn't see her go in, but I met her coming out and she was carrying the forms. And then one time while you were in the ladies' Sheila went in. I think she put something on your desk. She wasn't in there long, but her body blocked me from seeing what she actually did."

"Sheila?" Barbara grappled with the image of Sheila trying to incriminate her by putting the checks in her drawer. It didn't come together. Then she tried out Margie in the same vision but that didn't fall into place, either.

"I know. I can't believe anyone who works here would to that," Cindy said. "And I know that everyone thinks I'm the most logical suspect. I guess I understand why. But I'm not stupid enough to do something like that right after the Festival thing. I mean..." She stared down at her fingernails, her breath coming in harsh pants. "I've done some stupid things in my life. But doing this, now, would be insane."

"All right." Barbara said, though she wasn't sure she believed Cindy's protestations of innocence. "At this point, it's out of our hands anyway. The sheriff's department will have to sort it out. I think I'm still the main suspect. Those checks were in my desk."

"Maybe there's a way we can figure it out ourselves," Cindy suggested, sounding more hopeful than confident.

"Maybe, but I haven't any idea how right now." Nothing useful occurred to her the rest of that day or that evening, either.

Getting ready for work on Thursday morning, she pulled down the box holding her beige Stuart Weitzman pumps to go with her favorite black suit and off-white silk blouse. She couldn't say why she felt the need to be at her absolute best, but the itch nagged at her.

Something else niggled at her, too, something important, but it wasn't rising to the top of her brain yet.

At ten o'clock she learned why the need for sartorial reinforcement felt so strong. She answered the phone and a deep voice she didn't recognize said, "Miss Wilton? This is Sheriff Will McCormick. Can you come down to the station right away? We have some new information in the checks case."

Everything about his tone was neutral and professional, giving away nothing, but shivers ran up and down her spine. The fact they wanted her to come there didn't bode well. The demand, couched politely as a request, sounded downright ominous to her.

Something still niggled at her but refused to come together as she entered the police station and was directed to a conference room. The two men already there stood as she entered. One was a man of medium height with a wrestler's build and square face but sharp, intelligent eyes and a ready smile. He held out a hand to welcome her and said, "Thank you for coming, Miss Wilton. I'm Will McCormick, county sheriff."

"Pleased to meet you, Sheriff. At least, I hope I am."

He smiled but didn't answer. The other man in the room was Chris Harper.

The sheriff spoke first. "I was hoping I could ask you a few more questions, if I might."

She looked at Chris, but he met her gaze with a neutral expression that gave nothing away.

"Of course," she said.

He went through a series of questions about her work, her background, the reasons for her moving to Willow Ridge, her interests, hobbies, and even the car she drove. She answered as honestly as she could.

When he suggested that one of her employees had said she had expensive tastes, the pieces started to fall in place. Shock held her still for a moment, though, followed by dismay and sadness.

"Miss Wilton?" The sheriff broke into the reverie she'd fallen into. "Are you all right?"

"Yes. No. Maybe." She drew a deep breath. "May I ask who told you I had expensive taste? And did they by any chance use my shoes or purse as examples?"

"As a matter of fact, they did talk about your shoes. Some very expensive shoes you have by a fancy designer."

"I inherited some money from an aunt. Not a huge amount but enough to buy a few luxuries every now and then. Otherwise I live on my salary. I can prove it."

The sheriff gave her a pointed stare. "You don't need to. For the other question, I think you know the answer already."

Her voice shook. "There's only one other person in the office who would even recognize Stuart Weitzman shoes and a Kate Spade purse. I've been trying to put it together all morning. The shoes reminded me of something this morning when I put them on. Red soles on her heels one day when she was dressed up. The right shade of red."

"I'm sorry?" The sheriff looked confused.

"Christian Louboutin shoes always have

dark-cherry-red soles. And they're expensive. Really expensive. As much as a thousand dollars expensive. I don't know how she could afford them unless her husband has a high-paying job."

"He works for the electric company," McCormick said. "And he's Sam Russell's nephew."

She felt sick to her stomach. "You're sure of it?"

She looked from the sheriff to Chris. Both men wore grim expressions. The sheriff pulled out a phone and sent a text. A reply pinged within moments. "She's in the lobby. They're taking her to room one."

"Are you sure, though?" Barbara asked. "The connection with Sam Russell doesn't prove anything."

"We have a fingerprint, too," Chris said. "The check folder had been wiped clean so only your prints were on it. But we recovered a different print from one of the checks. It matches."

"Oh." Both men stood. The sheriff said, "Chris, if you would take Miss Wilton to observation?"

Chris led her down a couple of halls and around a bend to an area where they could see through what she assumed was a one-way window into a small room with a table and four chairs.

The door to the other room opened and the sheriff escorted Margie inside. "Come in, Mrs. Standish. Thank you for coming again so soon. Have a seat."

Margie sat down and looked around. "What can I do to help you?" she asked. "I answered all your questions the other day."

"We have a few more for you in light of some new information we have," McCormick said. "You told us that you hadn't been in Miss Wilton's office at all on Monday, but a witness tells us that you did in fact go in there early in the morning."

"Oh, right. I forgot about that. I needed some forms and was out of them at my station."

The sheriff nodded. "Can you explain why we found your fingerprint on one of the checks that were found in Miss Wilton's drawer?"

The color drained from Margie's face along with the pleasant expression. She stood abruptly and turned to leave. "I don't have to put up with these accusations. I came here on my own and now I'm leaving."

The sheriff stood and blocked her path to the door. "I'm afraid not," he said. "But you might want to call an attorney. We'll provide a phone for you."

Barbara's stomach wrenched and she turned away.

"Seen enough?" Chris asked.

She choked out a quick, "Yes."

He led her to a side door of the office that opened to a parking lot. She followed him around the building and down the street to the town square. They found a bench in a shady corner under a stand of trees. On a Thursday morning, only one mother with two children played there, but they were on the other side, well out of earshot.

"I'm sorry," he said, taking her hand after they'd settled down. "Sorry for all of it. Sorry that I had to abandon you. Sorry for the days of worry you've had. Sorry you had to witness that. Sorry you were betrayed by a co-worker." He shook his head and his mouth tightened. "Two co-workers, in fact. It killed me that I couldn't do anything to support or help you. My mother's been giving me a hard time about it, too, if it makes you feel any better. Another day or so and she'd probably stop speaking to me." He squeezed her fingers and his shoulders sagged. "I actually contemplated resigning from the force. The only thing that kept me from doing it was knowing I'd be even more helpless to do anything if Will did decide to charge you."

He turned toward her. Light filtering through the leaves fell across his face, showing a spark of—fear?—in his light blue eyes. "If you can't forgive me, let me know now and I'll walk away."

She reached out, put her hands on his upper arms and dragged him closer. "I'm not really into PDA. At least not usually, but I'm making an exception." She leaned in to kiss him, holding nothing back.

After a few minutes she pulled away and said, "I hope that answers the question?"

He was breathing hard. "I guess this means we might have a future?"

Happiness bubbled slowly from her heart to every part of her. "Less 'might have' and more 'future'. I hope."

"I do, too." Slow joy spread across features that had been gloomy and stern an hour ago.

"I'm not sure Mookie didn't miss you as much as I did," she admitted. "He's been kind of depressed the last few days, too." She held his hand. "By the way, I'm planning to call and tell the animal shelter that the fostering has failed. I'm adopting him. Will that be a problem for you?"

His grin showed adorable dimples. "I'll put up with a lot more than one big, klutzy canine if you're part of the deal." His expression went serious again. "I come with more baggage than just a dog, though. My mother and my Aunt Ruth are part of the deal, I'm afraid. It may turn out that they can manage to live on their own together, but maybe not."

"I absolutely insist on your mother being part of the deal," she said. "We make great shopping partners. And you haven't met my family in Boston yet. They might give you second thoughts."

"I'll deal with them."

"We'll need to stay in Willow Ridge for a while. I think I can settle down here, but I don't know if I want to stay forever."

"I don't know if I do either," he said. "As long as you're okay with staying for now, we'll manage the rest as it comes. Together. I suppose it's too soon to formally ask you to marry me. But I don't plan to wait long."

"Good."

They sat and talked for a while longer, making plans, enjoying each other's company and letting relief and joy sink into them. There was some kissing involved, too.

When her phone pinged with a text, she ignored it, but that real-world intrusion reminded her that it was still a work day. "I suppose I should be getting back to the bank," she said.

"And I'm still on duty."

Neither of them moved for a bit, reluctant to part, even for a short time.

Finally, he sighed and stood. "I'd better get back. But I'll come over this evening to apologize to Mookie in person. Then I'm taking you out for a nice dinner to celebrate."

Barbara stood as well. They kissed again before he turned to go.

"I'll be counting the minutes," she said.

EPILOGUE

The last baseball game of the season was that Saturday. Most of the other players were already there when Chris and Barbara drove up. She was surprised by how many people sat in the stands, too. Usually only a few dozen friends and family members of players showed up, but it looked like more than a hundred had come out for this. The thought of playing in front of a crowd intimidated her, but Chris threw an arm around her shoulders and said, "You'll do fine. We both will."

Tyler sought out Barbara as she got her mitt out of her bag.

"I've been practicing with my brother," he told her. "And ever since you helped with the follow-through, I've been getting better and better. Jay pitches for his high school team. I told him what you told me about reaching toward home plate. He's been practicing that, and he's getting better, too."

"That's good," Carl said, coming up behind her. "We're going to need you to pitch. Jeff can't make it tonight. Ryan's out, too." He looked at

Barbara. "How are you at first base?"

"Haven't played there in a long time but I guess I can handle it."

"Good." He hitched a quick breath. "There are some jerks on the other team and some of them may try to run you down. Just get out of the way. Don't need anybody getting hurt. Okay?"

"Not okay," she answered. "I'm not letting them intimidate me into ceding the base. But I don't plan to get hurt either. I'll work it out."

Carl looked around. "Chris? Come here and talk some sense into her."

Chris came over and Carl explained what he'd told her.

"She's probably the most sensible person I know," Chris said. "Except for that ruthless competitive streak."

"Hey," she said. "I resemble that remark."

"You do," the two men said together.

"Try to keep out of the way of trouble," Chris suggested.

For the first two hours, trouble stayed out of her way. Tyler threw a lot of strikes. Two balls went to the shortstop and were caught in the air for the automatic out. One was fielded by the second baseman and tossed to her for the out, but she snagged it well before the runner got close. The other two batted balls were caught in the outfield.

She recognized the other team's pitcher right away as the bully who'd tried to intimidate her at the Little League game the previous week. Tig something. He noticed her, too, and the narrowing of his eyes didn't portend good things. She struck out in her first at-bat in the second inning and hit a weak grounder in the fourth fielded by the shortstop who threw her out at first.

The game grew tighter when each team scored two runs in the sixth. They went into the seventh inning tied. She came up to bat third, with the two players ahead of her both getting outs. Tig, the pitcher, stared at her as she took her place in the batter's box.

She saw the intention in his eyes. She let herself grin, just a little, acknowledging the challenge. The first pitch was right over the plate for a strike. The second was inside, close to her body, but not by much. She swung at it and missed. As she expected, the third pitch flew by so close she had to jump back to avoid being hit. But she watched the man, studying his movements, how he started his windup and the way he finished. She backed off the plate a little for the next pitch, and he chased her, throwing even farther inside toward her, forcing her to step back again.

Out of the corner of her eye, she saw Carl stand up to protest, but she shook her head at him. He scowled, but she smiled in return. He got the message and backed off.

One more time to confirm her suspicion. This time the pitch was over the plate. She swung and fouled it off. On the next try, she saw the little hitch in his wind-up and where his eyes went right before he threw the ball. She stepped back to avoid it, and swung weakly, missing, for the final out in the inning.

When she walked back to the dugout, Carl confronted her. "What were you doing out there? You knew he was throwing at you."

"I was figuring out how we're going to win the game," she told him.

"What? Explain."

"Okay. Here it is. I'm a woman. I know I'm not as strong as you guys. I can't play harder, so I have to play smarter. I watch everything, and I notice details. Here's one thing I noticed. That pitcher, Tig Something? Watch where he holds the ball as he gets ready to wind up. If he has it right at his shoulder, he's going right over the plate, or at least trying for it. If he holds it by his ear, he's going to his right, inside on the right-handed batters. The higher he holds it, the farther off the plate he's going. Watch his face. He looks toward exactly where's going to throw it. If it's low, his whole face tilts down more. High and he's looking up more. Put those two together and you can pretty much figure out exactly where he's throwing."

"Hold up," Carl said. He signaled for the other players to huddle around them, and most did. Only the catcher, Jarrod, and a couple of others hung back. "Repeat that," he said.

The others listened. "I hope they keep him in for the rest of the game," one commented.

"I think he'll insist on it," Barbara said. "He still thinks he can nail me with a pitch. I toyed with him a bit, and I hope it made him think it was just luck that he didn't get me. He'll want to try again."

Carl looked at her with an odd expression. "Remind me to stay on your good side, lady."

She grinned and went to take her position on first base. Nothing much happened during that half inning, but when her teammates went up to bat, two of them got hits that gave them a one run lead in the game. In the top of the ninth, she finally had to field a ball at first, with a runner from the other team bearing down on her. He started to slide toward the base, cleats first, as she took the throw from the shortstop. The throw was low and short, forcing her to hop off the base to field it, but stepping forward protected her from being run over as well.

The runner was safe at first and she was still in one piece. Jarrod was furious and yelled something she couldn't quite make out. Just as well. She didn't really care. Two hitters later, Tyler gave up a double and the runner scored from first to even the score again.

In the bottom of the ninth Jarrod beat out a single to first, and Chris, hitting ahead of her, moved him to third with a nice line-drive double straight up the center. That brought her up to the plate. From third Jarrod yelled at her, "Don't mess it up, Wilton."

She raised her eyebrows at him but didn't say anything. As she expected, Tig still wanted to hit her, but he didn't want to load the bases either. She thought he'd settle for showing her up by blowing some wicked hard pitches past her. But she'd also noticed that when he tried to throw hard, he sent the ball high and right down the middle.

The first pitch came that way but even higher than she anticipated. She swung at it and missed. His setup told her the next ball would be inside. It came close to her, but she didn't offer at it. She read that the next would also be inside and prepared herself. She stepped back, letting her weight settle onto her right foot as she waited, watching the pitcher release the ball.

It arrived exactly where she anticipated. She swung the bat, shifting her weight forward, and connected right on the sweet spot. The ball sailed upward toward right center field, still gaining altitude as it went over the second baseman's head, then over the right fielder, who was running for all he was worth. She ran, too, but watched the ball's flight as she headed for first. She was just touching the bag when it flew over the fence.

Jarrod walked to home plate. Chris ran the bases quickly but realized as he approached home that he needn't hurry. She didn't even have to circle the bases, but she did, for the sheer joy of it. The players on the other team were already leaving the field by the time she reached home.

The entire team gathered there, but it was Chris who embraced her and lifted her off the ground in his exuberance. The next few minutes blurred in her memory. She heard the cheers and accepted the congratulations of team-mates. But all she really remembered was Chris holding her and how good that felt. The way he looked at her, the joy and pride in his expression. How much she wanted to stay in that moment.

Eventually he did set her down, though the cheers and congratulations continued for a while. They left the ballfield and went with some of the others to a local pub to celebrate. When someone offered a toast to her winning home run, even Jarrod reluctantly held up a glass in salute.

She blushed and looked around the room.

Georgia was there with some friends and stopped by a few minutes later to congratulate her on the good game and the relationship with Chris. "Looks like you get your own case of *Loving the Lawman*," she said. "I'm happy for both of you. By the way, next month's book club book is called *Love on Ice*. Edie is saving a copy for you."

ABOUT THE AUTHOR

Karen McCullough is the author of almost two dozen published novels and novellas in the mystery, romance, suspense, and fantasy genres, including the Market Center Mysteries Series, originally published by Five Star/Cengage and reprinted by Harlequin Worldwide Mystery Library, and three books in the No Brides Club series of romance novels. A member of Mystery Writers of America, Sisters in Crime, as well as local chapters of each, and the Short Mystery Fiction Society, she is also a past president of the Southeast chapter of Mystery Writers of America and served on the MWA national board.

Karen has won numerous awards, including the 2021 Bould Awards, an Eppie Award for fantasy, and has also been a finalist in the Daphne, Prism, Dream Realm, International Digital, Lories, and Vixen Award contests. Her short fiction has appeared in a wide variety of anthologies.

After fifteen years as a computer programmer/analyst, she made a career shift and spent ten years as an editor for two multi-national publishing companies, before retiring to start her own web design business. She lives in Greensboro, NC, with her husband of many years.

Website: http://www.kmccullough.com
Blog: http://www.kmccullough/kblog
Facebook:
https://www.facebook.com/KarenMcCulloughAuthor

SNEAK PEEK
FALLING FOR THE HOCKEY PLAYER

CHAPTER 1

Georgia Smith blew on the chocolate-speckled froth that graced the top of her coffee. The mug warmed her hands, like the heat which glared against the nape of her neck. Another warm day in August for Willow Ridge. Sitting outside may not have been her best decision, however it gave her breathing room away from prying eyes. The cafe windows glinted with the sun's rays, showcasing the cleaning she'd labored over the day before. It wouldn't do for Latte Da, the best coffee shop in town, to look anything but pristine.

Georgia took a tentative sip of her latest brew. The beans were rich and creamy, just as she preferred them. She hoped the customers of Willow Ridge would enjoy them, too. Last time she'd changed over to a new bean supplier the town had almost gone into meltdown. She'd learned her mistake there. Any changes to the cafe had to be gradual and spoon-fed.

Some folks just didn't like changes to their daily routines, a sentiment she could understand. Of late though, change was something she craved. Next month she'd turn thirty, and boy...how little she'd achieved with her life. All the dreams she'd had as a young girl and shared with her high school sweetheart whom she'd planned to marry? Not one achieved. Those dreams still lingered, floating in the back of her mind, but she'd not taken a single step toward them.

Georgia shifted in her chair, crossing one denim-clad leg over the over and bouncing her foot, the tassels on her sandals bobbling with the movement. Her eyes drifted over the front of the cafe. Duck-egg blue panels lined the window, which gave her a clear view into the shop. Millie Smith, her grandmother and Willow Ridge's unofficial town busybody, was behind the counter grinding the same beans Georgia was currently drinking.

Millie owned Latte Da, a gift from Georgia's grandfather before he'd died.

Georgia only worked there.

Her parents were off travelling around America, living the proverbial dream after running a successful real estate business half their lives.

Georgia lived in their pristine Georgian house.

Her sister was happily married to a doctor with a brood of talented kids, their oldest an up-and-coming ice hockey star.

Georgia was single. Still.

She fingered the dog-eared corner of the notebook that lay on the glass coffee table before her. Years of work, dreams, plans, and images cut and pasted and all stuck into this one journal. Blake had given it to her. Her heart issued a familiar pang of regret. She was the black sheep of the family, the one to break with the tradition of marrying one's childhood sweetheart and enjoying a blissful life thereafter.

Georgia's phone buzzed, breaking her from her thoughts.

"Hello, Georgia speaking." She threw fake brightness behind her tone.

"Georgia! I tried the line at Latte Da, but Millie said you were on a break. Can you collect Noah this afternoon?"

Georgia frowned. Her sister's voice held a note of panic, her words tumbling out in a confused array.

"Hi, Kaitlyn, how are you? I'm fine, thanks for asking," she replied with amusement. "Why would I be collecting Noah?"

A giant sigh heaved down the line, and Georgia gave the sky a gentle eye roll. Her sister was one for dramatics. Mind you, with five kids, a busy doctor for a husband, and running her own business, she was constantly juggling balls in the air, so perhaps some histrionics were natural.

Kaitlyn's voice came through the line again, though it was muffled. Her garbled words were hard to decipher, but when Georgia heard Pete—the dog's name—mentioned, she assumed that her sister wasn't talking to her anymore.

She raised a shoulder, locking her cell phone against her ear while she took another sip of her coffee. Maybe she needed to sell some of the beans to customers? It may help them get used to this new flavor. She was trialing them today, warning customers they were different beans, but the fact of the matter was the coffee had to change. The current supplier was hiking his prices—again—and that simply wouldn't work for Latte Da. It was a successful business, but only because Georgia made sure of it. Or Millie made sure of it. Georgia swallowed; it wasn't her coffee shop.

A thud sounded through the phone. "Georgie-pie, are you there?"

Georgia gritted her teeth, she hated her sister's pet name for her, not that she'd ever admit to disking it. It also meant her sister was about to ask a favor of her, one which Georgia knew she'd agree to.

"What do you need me to do for Noah?" She didn't attempt to hide her resignation.

"Sorry. I honestly thought I'd already spoken to you about this, but then Ryan reminded me this morning and said I hadn't. Honestly, I'm going to lose my head one of these days. Noah has been selected for the Savannah Pirates minor league ice hockey team! Isn't that just the sweetest? Anyhoo. He needs to be at the rink this afternoon to meet his coaches. There's some rumor of a National Hockey League player being there. Can you even imagine?"

Georgia swallowed; her stomach shimmied at the mention of the National Hockey League. Certainly, a place where dreams were made and broken.

"Georgia? Are you listening?"

"Yes, Kaitlyn. You need me to collect Noah and drive him into Savannah this afternoon. What time does his bus arrive from school? I'll tell Millie I need to leave Latte Da early."

"Three. He needs to be in Savannah at the rink by four. If you can maybe rustle him up some food before you take him? I know he just loves your peach pies. Though maybe nothing too unhealthy; he may have to skate. Ryan was

vague on the details for this afternoon's
meeting. I'm sorry to dump this on you. Ryan
was going to bring Noah himself; I mean gosh,
he's so proud of Noah for making the team.
Minor league hockey at seventeen, can you
imagine? His coach reckons he has a real shot
to make the draft in a year or two if he keeps
improving."

Kaitlyn paused and let out what could only
be described as a proud mom trill of laughter.

"Noah has worked very hard," Georgia
murmured when the pause extended. She
wasn't sure if Kaitlyn had become distracted
again or had been waiting for input into the
conversation.

"Oh, sweetheart, I must run. Pete's being
collected for a walk and my work line is ringing
off the hook. Thanks a bunch for agreeing to
this. I knew I could count on you."

Her sister hung up before Georgia had
managed half a goodbye. Her eyes were drawn
back to her journal. This morning she'd pulled
it out of its storage box at the back of her closet
on a whim. She hadn't look at it in months, but
something about the nearness of her birthday
had rattled her into action. Funny that she'd
thought of it today, only to have her sister
remind her of her ice hockey fascination shortly
after.

Not that she'd admit to still loving ice
hockey. These days she was limited to
experiencing it between the pages of the
romance novels she devoured. She wouldn't
allow herself to watch any of the actual games
or follow the league. It was too painful to see
Blake's familiar face plastered across the

screen.

He wasn't her destiny, even if years ago she'd desperately hoped he would be.

*

Noah was standing just beyond the bus stop, propped up against one of the French-style lampposts that lined the main street of Willow Ridge. Georgia pulled in against the curb and left the car running while she hopped out to help Noah with his bag. She needn't have bothered. Noah had an overnight duffle bag slung over his shoulder, and another small bag which she assumed held his skates. He gripped his hockey stick in his right hand.

"Hey Aunty G, thanks for doing this. I know mom sprung it on you."

She waved away his apology, instead enveloping him in a giant bear hug.

"You've grown taller," she muttered accusingly. She barely reached his shoulders these days, not that she was short herself.

"Yeah, mom says it's all the food I eat. Speaking of food, don't suppose you have any?" Noah's smile was the spitting image of Kaitlyn's. A smile Georgia had never been able to say no to.

"C'mon then. Put your stuff in the trunk, and we'll swing back past Latte Da. Grandma Millie will never forgive me if you don't pop in to say hi."

As predicted, Millie fussed over Noah the moment the doorbell tinkled, and they stepped through the front door.

"Noah my boy, look at you! What is Kaitlyn

195

feeding you down south."

Georgia clucked her tongue. "Millie, it's barely a twenty-minute drive to Kaitlyn's house from here. But as it happens, Noah did mention he had a hankering for pie."

"Serve up three plates of the pumpkin pie, Georgia. Now, Noah, I need to hear everything about this new coach. Maybe he's a looker and could catch Georgia's eye. She's getting long in the tooth."

A sigh slipped out, and Georgia attempted a cough to hide it. Marrying young and staying married was a Smith family trait. One that appeared to skip Georgia. She had managed the engagement part at eighteen and had been blissfully happy for a few glorious weeks.

"Georgia, the pie?" Millie said, nodding with enthusiasm.

Georgia walked behind the counter and pulled the pan from the corner refrigerator. The pumpkin pie was just the right shade of burnt orange, flecked with black clove speckles. She drank in the rich smell, knowing it would taste even better than it looked. Having worked through lunch, she served herself and Noah slightly larger portions than she normally would and added a dollop of whipped cream.

"Here you go," she said, delivering all three plates at once.

"So, who is the new coach, Noah? Or have you covered that already?" Georgia asked, before popping her first mouthful in. The creamy texture and hints of cinnamon and nutmeg sang on the back of her tongue. She might be a failure in most aspects of her life, but boy, could she make pie.

"I don't know. There was some talk of a new coach, but Dad said this morning that Gareth is still running the show for the Savannah Pirates."

Gareth Thompson, another reminder from her past. Gareth had been Blake's coach back when they were young, and Blake had still lived in Willow Ridge...

Millie licked the last crumb off her spoon. "What are these rumors I hear about a National Hockey League player coming to Savannah, then?"

Georgia stilled, holding her breath and waiting for Noah to answer.

"It's just a rumor, but one of my teammates reckons he knows who it is."

Georgia choked on a mouthful. The fudge-like texture of pie filling clung to the back of her throat, and she gasped, attempting to dislodge it. "Did he say who?" she whispered, her eyes watering as Millie slapped a hand between her shoulder blades. She cleared her throat and nodded to Millie to indicate she had recovered. "Is he still playing for the NHL?"

"Such interest, Georgia," Millie quipped. Her eyes held a tell-tale twinkle that caused Georgia to cringe internally. She'd seen that look before, and it had resulted in her being coerced into one of the worst blind dates ever. Dating vicariously through her romance books and her imagination was her preferred method these days.

"Can't an aunt be interested in her nephew's sporting pursuits?" She spooned up the last bite of her pie and quickly shoveled it in, hoping it would stop her asking any more questions in front of her grandmother. Millie wouldn't put family before gossip, though it was all done with love. There'd be time on the twenty-minute drive to Savannah to grill Noah for more information.

Georgia was letting her imagination run away with all this talk of the National Hockey League and mentions of possible visitors. It was probably just a rumor to increase interest in the local team. She never should have opened her old journal; it was making her remember parts of her life that were best left taped shut.

She was making up fairy tales. She put that down to last night's meeting of her book club, the Hopeless Romantics of Willow Ridge, as they called themselves who met at the local bookstore. Each month a book was chosen by the book store's owner, Edie Rogers. This month's book was Love on Ice, a sweet ice hockey romance. Just because the previous books chosen had led to certain book club participants finding love with similar heroes didn't mean a single thing. It didn't mean that this month it would be her time to find love. Edie just loved to pick romance tropes that appealed to all of them.

"You two had better get your skates on if your meeting is at four," Millie spoke, collecting up the scraped clean plates. Noah caught Georgia's eye, who was trying not to laugh at the pun.

Georgia smiled back, used to being mollycoddled by Millie. "Okay, Millie. Thank you for stepping in this afternoon. I'll swing past to tally up today's earnings and prep baking for tomorrow when we get back."

Millie waved them away. "You do what you need to, Georgia. I know I can depend on you to keep my Latte Da running smoothly."

Georgia held her smile in place, but her grandmother's words shot her back to her uneasy feelings from this morning. The only thing Georgia owned that was fully hers was her car. At nearly thirty, what did that say about her?

]

Hopeless Romantics of Willow Ridge Series

Can a group of hopeless romantics finally find love? Or are they destined always to be a bridesmaid and never the bride?

Falling for the Boss,
Book 1 – Raine English

Tally Turner lost her fiancé and business in one fell swoop. While picking up the pieces of her shattered life, she promises herself two things: to never fall in love again and to keep her private life and career separate. No exceptions. However, she made the promise before she met her gorgeous new boss.

Jack Barre is tired of women wanting one thing from him—his money. So he leaves the bright lights of New York City for the small Southern town of Willow Ridge and plans to concentrate solely on making his latest business venture a success. Little does he know that he's about to meet a woman who will turn his world upside down and cause him to second guess everything.

Will Tally and Jack overcome the past and risk it all for love?

Falling for the Fireman
Book 2 – Monique McDonell

Bronte Fishburn loves her hometown of Willow Ridge and her job as an elementary school teacher, but she wishes she could find someone to spend her life with. Someone who loves this town and wants to settle here as much as she does. She used to dream that someone would be her neighbor Ben, but he left her behind years ago and it's time she created a new dream. Except now Ben is back, sleeping in her spare room and a constant reminder of what she can't have.

Firefighter Benjamin Wakefield vowed never to return to Willow Ridge. But his grandfather needs his help to clean out his house and move to a retirement community, so after ten years away he's back in a town that seems unchanged. Another thing that hasn't changed are his feelings for Bronte, who is brighter and more beautiful than the day he left. But she's still too good for him and he's still not planning to stay. He needs to resist the urge to ignite that growing spark between them to be the good guy she thinks he is.

Is the pull between Ben and Bronte enough to build a future on?

Falling for the Doctor
Book 3 – Cindy Ray Hale

Abby Cameron is barely holding it together. She's a single mom, farmhand, and a home health aide to her ailing, widowed grandfather. The last thing she needs is for her daughter to get constantly sick. At least her daughter's pediatrician is easy on the eyes. She can't help her growing attraction to him. After the dark past Abby's had with her cheating ex, she's sure she'll never trust again. But maybe Dr.

Howard will have the power to not only help her heal her daughter with his medical knowledge, but to also help Abby's heart to mend from her painful past.

When Abby's daughter comes down with an ear infection yet again, Dr. Matthew Howard doesn't expect to end the appointment teamed up with Abby to compete in the town's talent show. He's not sure it's the best idea since he's so attracted to her. After all, his heart is empty after the tragic death of his fiancée from cancer. But as he spends more time with his little patient and her beautiful mother, he wonders if having a family might be in his future. He's just not sure he can allow someone into his heart after experiencing so much loss.

Falling for the Deputy
Book 4 – Karen McCullough

After losing at love twice, Barbara Wilton needs a change, some place far from her home in Boston, so she takes a position as manager of a small branch bank in Willow Ridge, Georgia. She's done with relationships and ready to concentrate on her career. The experience in Willow Ridge will help her move forward in the banking industry, but she doesn't plan to stay there permanently. Nevertheless, an invitation to join the Hopeless Romantics book club, a position on a planning committee, helping a little league team that needs coaching, and being adopted by a stray dog begin to wind her into the community.

Chris Harper was a police officer in Charlotte until his marriage fell apart. With his mother and elderly aunt in deteriorating health, Chris returns home to Willow Ridge to help them and takes a job as chief deputy to the local sheriff. The wound left by his failed marriage is still raw and, despite his mother's nagging, he's not interested in pursuing any relationship, even with the attractive new bank manager.

Fate, helped by a few local residents, conspires to push Barbara and Chris together. They meet during a false alarm at the bank and then he assists her with a car problem. But when his aunt receives a foreclosure notice on her house, Chris is angry with Barbara for not warning him that his aunt was behind on her payments.

She agrees to help him work out the problem with the bank, but the deeper issues between them keep flaring. Can two wary, wounded people learn to trust again and find happiness together?

Falling for the Hockey Player
Book 5 – Jayne Kingsley

Georgia Smith is a small-town girl with small town dreams. Once upon a time she wished for more but that was before she let fear drive away the love of her life. Now, she works in her grandmother's coffee shop, vicariously experiences romance in books and resides in her parents' old house. Even her dog isn't her own. Enough is enough, it's time to start a new chapter, a goal just for her. If only she knew what that was...

Blake Bishop's life is ice hockey. His dream of winning the Stanley Cup was right within his grasp when an unlucky hit slapped it away. Now he's back in Savannah, Georgia, hiding from the world and trying to sort out his next steps. Will coaching the small-town team where he grew up be enough or is it just a reminder of all he's lost?

Blake and Georgia have a past that can't be forgotten. When their paths cross, they realise that perhaps what is really holding them back, is the lack of each other in their lives. If only they can forget the past.

Falling for the Single Dad
Book 6 – Christina Butrum

Jayda Thompson is passionate about her career in New York City after being promoted to an Online Marketing Specialist. She knows marketing inside and out and is more than ready to take on new clients. However, her excitement fades into uncertainty when her boss closes the business for the last quarter of the year. She agrees to take a much-needed vacation and visit her grandmother in the small Southern town of Willow Ridge.

Scott Meyers is a single father who owns Meyers Realty in the heart of the small town. He wants nothing more than to give his daughter everything while trying his best to make ends meet. When he's given an opportunity to sell Once Upon a Book to a businessman in New York City, he plans to do whatever it takes to talk Edie Rogers into selling it. Little does he know that he's about to meet a woman who will make him question what life in a small town is all about.

Will Jayda and Scott put their differences aside and agree to meet in the middle?

Falling for the Farmer
Book 7 - Lindsay Detwiler

Ellie Mae Harding went to California to pursue two dreams: fashion and love. When she flunks out of fashion school and her boyfriend dumps her, though, she returns to her hometown feeling like a failure. The small southern town is a big change from her city dreams, especially since her parents own a farm. As she tries to find herself again in the middle of her shattered career and broken heart, she swears she won't let love ruin her dreams this time around. When she joins a book club in town to try to make friends, though, she might just change her mind about everything.

Trent Weston was a player in high school with a bad boy reputation. He abandoned the family business at eighteen to chase the open skies in Colorado. A family tragedy, though, has brought him home to Willow Ridge. When he starts working at a local farm, the boss's daughter catches his eye and makes him realize that the small town might not be so boring after all.

Will Trent and Ellie Mae heal each other's hearts, or are their restless spirits and big dreams too much for one relationship to handle?

Falling for the Scotsman
Book 8 – Jean C. Gordon

Sorcha Laurent's family-owned distillery has become her whole life. A far cry from where she'd expected to be when she'd left school with her newly minted MS in Chemistry and a sparkling new engagement ring on her finger. The family-business emergency that brought her home to the small-town of Willow Ridge has cost her a fiancée and her dream job in medical research. Now she's at the end of the five-year agreement to manage the family distillery. Sorcha is ready to get back to having a life of her own. It's time to throw in the bar towel and figure out what new dream might replace the one she lost. Little does she suspect that dream might involve potential business rival and swoon-worthy scholar, Ross Campbell.

A former Scotland National Rugby team player Ross Campbell is on track to his dream job, a professorship at his alma mater Edinburgh University. All he has left is to finish his doctoral thesis, while earning a few bonifieds as a history teacher at an exclusive boys school outside Savanah. The fact that people here in the States accept him for himself, not as a former rugby star nor an heir to the Campbell Beverage conglomerate, is only frosting on the cake. And there's no overbearing grandfather around pushing him to join the family corporation. Ross expects all things to continue according to plan, but meeting fiery Sorcha draws him down an unexpected and surprisingly enjoyable path.

When Ross catches Sorcha's eye at the

Savanah Scottish Games because he looks just like her historical romance book boyfriend, little do they know where their chance meeting will lead. A 50-year-old connection between her grandmother and his grandfather. A centuries-old mystery about a rumored stolen whisky recipe. Feelings that neither have experienced before and don't know how to handle.

Will Sorcha and Ross's research sessions take them beyond solving the recipe mystery and their intertwined ancestry to true love? Can they break free of family obligations and interference to live their dreams in a future together?